# UNYIELDING

## DEATH AND DEVOTION
## BOOK ONE

## LEILA THORNE

eBook ISBN: 978-1-7643557-2-8

Paperback ISBN: 978-1-7643557-3-5



No part of this book nor the author used Generative AI in its creation.

Edited by Bonnie from www.editsbybonnie.com

Cover Design by Quirky.Circe

www.leilathorneauthor.com

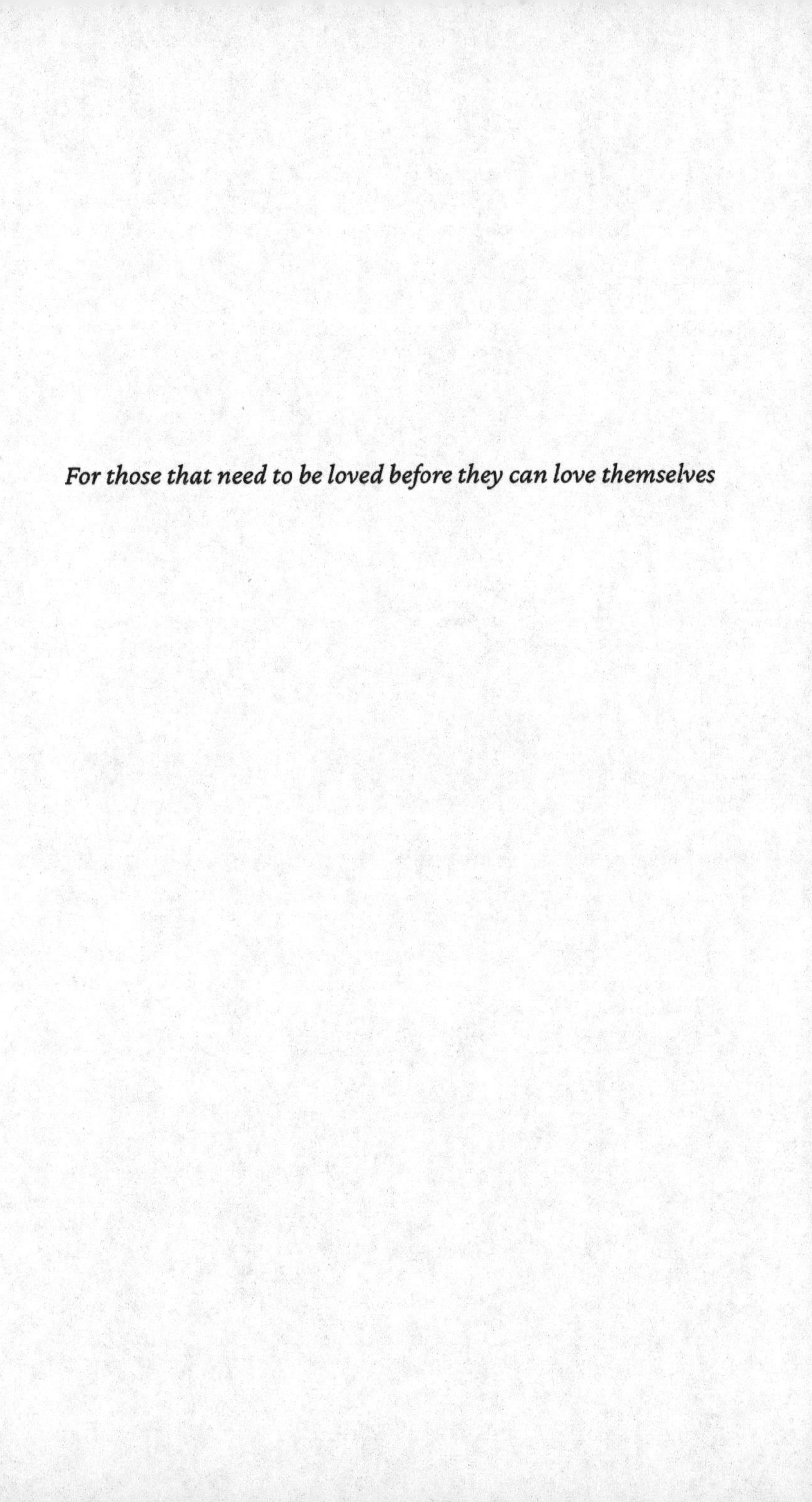

*For those that need to be loved before they can love themselves*

# CONTENT WARNING

Before you join me in this journey, you should know this is a dark romance. Please read at your own discretion but above all, protect your peace.

In this book you will find:

- Sexual assault
- Reference to sexual assault of a minor (off page)
- Physical Restraint
- Domestic violence
- Revictimisation
- Consensual non-consent
- Praise
- Squirting
- Foot play
- Body worship
- Gun violence
- Stalking
- Murder
- Descriptions of blood

- Torture
- Sexual assault with an object
- Mutilation
- Remote-controlled toys
- Light BDSM
- Branding via tattoo
- Graphic sex scenes
- Sex work
- Edging

# 1
# VALENTINA

The music was blaring, the air was thick with the smell of alcohol, sweat and smoke. The Velvet Room was one of many slightly unsavoury family businesses we owned but by far a cut above the rest. This little gem of a sex club was owned by my brothers but operated by my second-oldest brother, Zane. The man was slightly unhinged, with tastes to match. I usually kept myself removed from the family's businesses—being the youngest, a woman and not interested in contributing in any other meaningful way, my value lay in my ability to be sold off like chattel to form alliances in this ever-violent underworld we lived in.

Tonight wasn't about me though; it was about my best friend, Matt. He was getting married and this was how he decided to send off his single years—by being gyrated on by a throng of almost-naked women on the more muted level of the club, which was strictly reserved for erotic dances. Ashleigh, his bride-to-be, would have castrated him if he'd even thought about seeking out one of the upper levels, where almost anything was permitted. Walking towards the back, I found Matt sitting in a booth surrounded by some of his friends. Where Matt was a gentle giant, Tim was an awkward gamer guy Matt had gone to university with. Andrew, who sat at the end of the table, was a creep in every sense of the word and had been banned from nearly every club in the city. The only reason he was allowed inside these walls was that he was far too scared of my brother to try his usual antics—lest he felt suicidal.

I greeted Matt, as always, with a slight nod, paying no mind to the other two. They were his friends, not mine, and they were far too scared of my family to bother trying to form any kind of friendship with me. Matt and I had fallen into an unexpected friendship with him, having been the son of one of our housekeepers. When we first started earning real money and bought our home ten years ago, he became a sort of third brother, given that we were the same age.

Matt and I considered each other blood in every meaningful sense of the word. We had tried to make that a reality as kids when we were sixteen, slicing open our hands and shaking over a single oath. Now, at the age of twenty-five those scars served as a reminder of our vow to one another.

*Nothing and no one.*

It meant that quite literally nothing and no one else would ever come between our bond. No matter where we were dragged in life or the paths we decided to take, we would always be in each other's lives and have each other's backs. We were naïve to the realities of the world and as the years wore on, our lives began to centre around different things and different people but we still remained each other's anchor. Always there if we needed someone who understood.

'Hey V, going to get a dance tonight?' Matt asked with a

smirk. He knew this was not something I enjoyed and that I was only there to support him and throw back free drinks. Shaking my head, he laughed at my reluctance.

'This kind of thing isn't my scene.'

'Come on, you should know better than most that these girls want to be here.'

'*Women* Matt, they're not girls.' He dipped his head in embarrassment, nodding an apology my way.

I did know though. My brother Zane opened this place as a refuge for the women who were being drugged, abused and taken advantage of across the rest of the city. One by one, my family shut down every club in the city and opened this monster. It was five levels of sex and sin, built on a lack of inhibitions. The women set their own hours, own boundaries and own rates. My brothers barely got a cut compared to what most clubs had taken. They created a safe space for these women to partake in this line of work without fear. Security was better than anything any politician would have on their roster and ten times as vicious. Zane was known across the city for his particular brand of violence when the less-than-intelligent decided to cross him or anyone he considered family. And every one of these girls became family the moment he took them in.

Zane had bought the building across the road and converted it into apartments with twenty-four-hour child-care on-site. Not one of them paid childcare fees or rent; he funded the entire thing out of his own pocket. It was his version of repentance for his sins. There was a counsellor on standby at any time of day or night, and every person who worked here, whether they were a dancer, escort, bartender, or cleaner, had their education fully paid for. It was a safe haven in every sense of the word. He viewed himself as a blight on this world and this was how he made up for what he did in the shadows.

The great care he took with the people that worked in the Velvet Room translated into a lively, energetic and passionate atmosphere. There was life breathed into every square inch of this building. I had been to other clubs in the past for similar events. You could feel nothing but depression, fear and despair rolling off the bodies and walls of those places.

Matt grabbed my hand and pulled me to one of the secondary stages, sliding out a chair for me to sit in. There was a pale, lithe thing dancing on a pole, with long black hair trailing down to her lower back. Matt called her to the edge of the stage, whispered something into her ear, then handed her a bill. I couldn't help but roll my eyes at him as she raised her gaze to meet mine, before nodding and moving back to the centre of the stage.

Matt walked away with a wink thrown my way as the dark-haired dancer dropped to the floor of the stage and crawled towards me, spreading her legs and leaning into me in time with the music.

'What's your name?' she asked in that same purr all these girls had for their clients. It was a forced sensual tone that just wasn't believable to me. But to the average man, I'm sure they lapped it up, thinking their mere presence alone was enough to sexually undo these women.

'It's V,' I answered. She gave me her stage name, one I didn't bother to memorise. *Nova? Aurora?* Something galaxy-themed. As she focused her dance on me, my eyes stared at the shuttered look in her eyes. She seemed bored. She could have been scrolling on her phone for all her face let on, while her body moved as though she was thrumming with passion. I just couldn't grasp the clear disconnect. I sat there wondering what the men in my life found so fascinating about these places and these women.

When her dance ended she sat herself on the edge of the stage and asked if I wanted a more private dance. I pulled one hundred dollars from my bag and passed it to her as I shook my head no and returned to the boys.

Matt raised a brow in question as to why I didn't go with the dancer, but I merely shrugged. I stood on the edge of the table, barely paying attention to the conversation, making noises of agreement here and there to act as though I was engaged in whatever asinine thing they were discussing. I felt slightly guilty for being here and being miserable, but Matt knew me well enough by now that he never took my displeasure about being surrounded by people personally.

It wasn't long before another dancer made her way to the table. She was tall, with legs that seemed to go on for days. She wore a red lace set that crossed around her ribs to her back. As she made her way around the table to speak to Andrew, her tight, short curls bounced with every step; the lights reflected off the bleached ends that faded into dark brown roots. She leaned over the table to show case her red lace wrapped breasts while I absorbed the caramel colour of her skin that glistened with a light sheen of sweat. My mouth dried, and the sudden urge to lick my lips overwhelmed me. This was new; perhaps I was no better than the men who came here.

Andrew was holding out for a set of twins who were wrapping up a dance, so he wasn't interested in the dancer in front of us. Tim shook his head no as soon as she stepped towards him; he looked ready to hurl, having had one too many whiskeys. I could see Matt's knee bouncing under the table and knew, as soon as she approached him, that he was too far gone, craving a cigarette, to be able to sit through a dance.

She turned to address the boys, seeming not to bother with me yet.

'Come on, boys, don't you want to have a little fun tonight? I promise to make it worth your while,' she said in the most chipper tone I had ever heard in an environment such as this. She was practically thrumming with positive energy, a bright smile plastered on her face that met her deep brown eyes and appeared genuine, even in the face of multiple rejections. Something about her energy pulled at me. Matt was about to reject her once again, but I interrupted him by stepping in front of her.

'How about me?' Matt looked as shocked as I felt, but something about her trying so hard made it almost unbearable for me to watch her crash and burn, flailing in a sea of rejection. I wanted to preserve a piece of her dignity so she wouldn't have to beg. She didn't deserve that.

Her smile somehow grew brighter as she grabbed my hand and pulled me through a hallway that led to back rooms with only curtains for doors. She poked her head in a few, trying to find one that was empty. She joked that they seemed to be extra busy tonight; it was a Saturday night and we were not the only bachelor party in attendance. Pulling me deeper towards the back, she found one that was free, dragging me into it. She pushed me down into the black leather chair and closed the curtain behind her.

I took in every last detail of her as she stood over me, that caramel skin, her long legs and that face. She had sharp features accompanied by a bright smile, plump lips, and soft, endless brown eyes.

'Tell me the rules. What can I, and what can't I, do or

touch?' I said, wanting to make sure I didn't cross any boundaries in an effort to set her at ease.

'You can touch me anywhere except for my breasts and pussy,' she said, leaning in towards me. 'Now tell me what you like.'

Truthfully, I didn't know what I liked. This was new to me, as I had never had a private dance before, but instinctively, the words flowed out of me. 'I have no interest in your arse; perfect as it may be, it doesn't really do anything for me. I like the front of you more, but I like your face most of all.'

She stood there staring for a moment, having been thrown by a statement I doubt she had ever heard within these walls before, considering that most of the dancers' go-to move was to grind their arse on everyone. Maybe it made the job more tolerable not having to look them in the eyes, perhaps they felt less exposed but I wanted to strip this girl bare and not literally. I wanted to see everything that was inside of her, down to her core. I wanted to know how she made that smile reach her eyes each and every time.

Recovering quickly, she flashed that genuine smile of hers that lit up her face and left a twinkle in her eyes. The music changed and morphed into something slower and sexier as she began to move in rhythm with it. No person had ever been able to hold my attention in this way; it's why I never really dated, let alone spoke to anyone of either sex. But right now, I was ensnared by every movement of her body.

My eyes locked on her face as she danced over me, and the moment hers met mine, I couldn't look away. I was transfixed. The music faded, her dancing becoming irrelevant as her eyes captivated and held mine. I didn't know if I was even blinking at this point. My breathing turned ragged as I fell into those dark brown depths. At some point she had stripped out of her red lace lingerie but I didn't spare a glance for her naked body; instead I held her gaze as those eyes stoked a fire I hadn't ever felt within me.

She sunk down onto the floor and crawled towards me, pulling herself up and onto me by my legs until she was straddling my hips. Pressing her body against mine I felt her breathing turn heavy. Panting through the tension that had only built from how fiercely our gazes were locked.

Only one thought replayed in my mind over and over again. *I want her.*

'What's your name?' I asked, needing to know her, to unravel a piece of her, as I started to feel raw from what she was stirring within me.

'Sunshine,' she said, smiling even brighter. How fitting that name was, but something in my chest panged over the fact that I knew it wasn't her real name. This was a job, but to me, this moment—this tension, the look in her eyes that matched my own—felt so fucking real.

As she swayed her hips while straddling me, I brought my hands to the outside of her thighs, holding her steady. I couldn't help moving my hips in time with her, and before I could register what was happening, we were writhing against each other.

'Oh god, what is happening? You're making me blush,' she said, seemingly flustered as she panted, trying to gasp for more air as we moved as one. Taking my hand off her hip, I extended my finger. I had long, pointed nails that shimmered with a gold that matched the blonde in her hair. I placed the tip of my nail at the base of her throat and dragged it down her body, between her breasts, along her sternum and down her stomach. Her grip on my shoulders tightened as she drew me closer, swaying her hips as if she were riding me, losing control at my touch.

She held her lips just millimeters above mine as we stared into each other's eyes, our bodies moving as one in the most intimate of ways. Tension building to indescribable levels, I needed more.

'I want to bite you,' she breathed.

'Do it.' She shook her head at the challenge.

'I can't; they have rules on this level. I'll get fired. But I want to sink my teeth into you so badly.' She obviously had no idea who I was and that my family owned The Velvet Room.

'We can't have that now, can we?'

She must've been relatively new because I knew for a fact that my brother wouldn't punish her so severely for breaking a rule like that, and all it did was spark curiosity within me. *How long had she worked here? Where did she come from? How long had she been in this line of work?* I wanted to know everything about her and lick whatever wounds had sent her here.

My hands travelled to her sides as I gripped her waist, tracing them around to her back. Gazes locked I dragged my nails down her back and watched as she shivered beneath my touch. Once I got to her lower back the breath she was holding came out in a ragged gasp. That was all the encouragement I needed as I leisurely drew them back up her sides then across her shoulders. I bit my lower lip, trying to rein in the need that was taking over me as my body responded to every movement of hers. The look she gave me almost turned me feral; her eyes locked on my lips before meeting my gaze once more. She pressed her hips against mine harder than before. I sunk my nails deeper this time, and as I dragged them across her flesh, pleasure erupted from her in soft little pants than matched my own.

The music slowed and it marked the end of our private dance. The moment was ending but the tension refused to break between us.

I slid her a couple hundred dollars and thanked her for her time.

'I'm going to have to go to the employee lounge and cool down after that. You are so freaking hot,' she said as she stood and began putting her red lingerie back on. Something about that left me feeling satisfied that perhaps it was as real for her as it was for me, that she wasn't just incredibly good at her job.

'Good,' I said, smirking as I left the room and refusing to break eye contact until the curtain closed behind me. It wasn't long until I found Matt sitting by himself, watching one of the shows on the main stage. A girl was pouring champagne down her breasts and naked body.

'How was your first lap dance?' he asked, grinning at me.

'I think I'm in love,' I sighed. He coughed, choking on his whiskey at the ridiculous statement I just made.

'What's her name?' he asked.

Grinning back at him, I tasted her name on my lips for the first time.

'Sunshine.'

# 2

# SUNSHINE

I almost stumbled into the employee lounge. I felt flushed and hot. Looking at myself in the mirror as I braced against the sink, I saw the wild, heated look in my eyes. Splashing some cold water on my face and neck, I tried to cool myself down. Never had anyone made me feel anything remotely like this, and definitely not a woman. I had been dancing for years at various venues. I had danced for men and women of every age and from every walk of life, but never had someone ignited something so primal and instinctual in me. I wasn't dancing with her; I was trying to have sex without truly touching.

I didn't even know her name; all I knew was that when I looked into the depths of her dark brown eyes, I felt like I was freefalling, and she was my tether, making sure I didn't fully lose myself. Nova walked into the bathroom behind me. I had noticed her dancing on the mini stage earlier, trying to entice the woman who had me so flustered into a private dance. She wasn't interested, and some small part of me was immensely satisfied that she had chosen me.

'What are those marks?' she asked, walking closer to

my back. Turning to the mirror, I saw long red lines trailing down my back from her nails. She'd left a mark on me, one that would eventually fade, but for some reason, I didn't want it to. I wanted her to brand me. Surely, I must be ovulating, as I bordered on insanity with these hormones coursing through my body.

'Seems I know how to pull the clients you can't,' I said, smirking. Nova and I had a healthy competition going, but there was no bad blood between us.

'Bitch.' She chuckled. 'Just be careful the boss doesn't see those. Only the girls upstairs can be marked and only on their terms.' Zane was a terrifying boss, and I was glad he enjoyed the more depraved curiosities of the other levels. I couldn't imagine dancing for him. We all knew he would never cross a line with any of us; he did his best to protect each of us. But if there was anyone I had ever thought was born of the devil, it would be him. Everyone knew his reputation outside these walls and those of the De Luca family. It was part of the reason we felt so safe here; he instilled true primal fear throughout the entire city.

I found myself back downstairs, combing through the crowd as music blared from the speakers. A few men approached me but I didn't feel like accepting any of their invitations; I was still coming down from the tension of the last dance and frankly didn't want anyone else's paws on me, touching the marks she had left behind. They were mine and mine alone.

It wasn't long before one of the men who had been at her table earlier stopped me.

'Sunshine, was it?' he asked, holding out a hand to shake mine. It was an odd gesture, but I didn't mind it, knowing I had obviously left enough of an impression that she remembered the name I had given her and even talked about me with her friends.

'Yeah, and what's yours big guy?' I crooned, playing the part and immediately regretting it. It felt wrong.

'It's Matt,' he said matter of factly, not engaging with my hapless attempt at fake flirting.

'And why are you here, Matt? What can I help you with tonight?'

'I'm here for my bucks, but what I really want from you is to make sure my best friend over there has a great time,' he said, pointing behind us.

As I turned, I locked eyes with my mystery girl. Immediately, her eyes heated as they took me in before turning into a look of confusion as she surveyed the scene in front of her, with Matt holding onto my arm. She was on us in moments, subtly turning me towards her and pulling me from her friend's grasp.

'Well, what do we have here?' she asked, cocking a brow at me but talking to her friend.

'I think I'm owed a dance; it's my night, after all,' he said, challenging her.

'Are you paying?' she asked. Matt laughed, shaking his head.

'Go find someone else then; here's some cash,' she said, pulling out a thick wad of cash, which left me intrigued and wondering what she did for a living.

'But I want this one.' He pouted, pointing to me.

'Fuck you, Matt. If you want her, then we're sharing; you don't get her to yourself, especially if it's my money.' She stepped forward, grabbing me by my hand and pulling me towards one of the back rooms, with Matt trailing behind us. Once we were surrounded by curtains, I took the lead. I knew where I wanted to take them—my favourite room, filled with mirrors.

I normally didn't mind private dances with multiple clients; it broke it up and made the time go quicker. But right now, I wanted to be alone with the woman, and I knew I would struggle to share my time evenly between the two.

It was a larger room than the one I had her in before; on each end was a leather chair, with a mirror spanning across the wall from floor to ceiling. Turning my attention to the man of the hour as the song started, I stalked towards him while my eyes drifted to the gorgeous brunette sitting opposite us.

'Let's start with you, shall we, big boy? Let me give you the attention you deserve before I get a touch distracted,' I said while slowly peeling my eyes off of her relaxed body and onto him. It was a struggle. The entire time I danced with him, my eyes were fixed on hers. Turning around, I gyrated my hips on his lap and leaned back into the crook of his neck. She didn't look at my body like all the others; no, she watched my face just like last time.

'You can go to her if you want,' he said, watching me watch her, knowing I wasn't quite into dancing with him. He didn't seem bothered, more amused than anything and like he had been expecting this. Without a second thought, I stood and walked towards her, shedding my red lace and dropping it onto the floor. As I neared her, I felt the world fade away. Nothing else mattered.

'I'm glad we got this room; it's my favourite. I thought you would like the show in the mirror,' I purred.

'Now you'll get to feel me while you see everything, and I know you're not a butt girl, but trust me when I say the view is to die for.'

She raised a brow curiously as I dropped to the ground on all fours in front of her. I drew her leg towards me, pulling my body up as I dragged my lips and tits over the skin of her bare leg. She liked that. I could tell by the way her knees tried to close, clenching at the feeling it gave her. As the music continued, I stood and straddled her, throwing my legs on each side of her hips as I swayed in time with the music.

Her sinful nails drew themselves up my back again until they found their way into the back of my hair, trailing along my scalp, sending shivers up my spine. Slowly, she drew me closer until I was a breath away from her lips, and without thinking, I uttered the stupidest words.

'Your breath smells divine.' *Kill me now. What is wrong with me?* All I could think was that she smelled sweet and I wanted a taste. Before I knew it, I was uttering complete unsexy nonsense. She didn't seem dissuaded, though, as a smirk crept along her lips. She knew what thoughts had led to that confession.

'I taste even better,' she purred and it went straight between my legs, making me clench with want. I didn't think I'd ever have to fear becoming wet in this role, but here I was, worrying that the gushing need that consumed me with those words would become visible.

As I danced, the leather chair tipped slightly as one of its legs raised into the air. Momentarily, I froze, but her arms wrapped around my waist, holding me in place.

'Don't worry, I've got you,' she purred, reassuring me. I nearly lost my mind in that moment; I needed a minute to regroup after that.

Standing, I moved back to her friend and danced on him some more, never taking my eyes off of her as she continued to stare at me. It made me feel even hotter.

Wanted. More than I've ever felt before. I saw a flicker of jealousy; she truly didn't want to share and that thrilled me to no end.

Pulling myself off of her friend earlier than I should have, I found my way back to her. This time, I faced the mirror as I laid back against her. The reason I loved this room was the display in the mirror but when I looked there, I noticed her gaze wasn't on the mirror; instead, it was on the side of my face. She didn't care about my pussy on display or my body, instead she was enraptured by me.

Turning my head, I faced her, and our eyes locked once again in a battle of tension and heat. As I writhed on top of her, she writhed underneath me as her left hand slid over my side, down my stomach and settled on the skin just above my core. In rhythm with her hips that moved under me, I met her pace as her fingers stroked just above my slit, teasing at what I could have if she dipped her fingers just a couple of inches lower.

Her right hand wrapped around my throat and instead of panicking like I would with any other client, it sent shivers down my spine and wetness down my slit. I lost myself in the movement, shutting my eyes.

'God, what I would do to you,' she breathed into my ear. My eyes snapped open.

'God, what I would let you do to me,' I replied, needing her to believe I was right there with her in this moment and in the fantasies that this moment between us was conjuring.

The music faded, marking the end of our time together. As her friend nodded and left, she stood up to go, but I wasn't ready for her to leave.

'Stay, please. I want you to watch me put my lingerie

back on.' I gave her my hand to pull her up as she got to her feet.

'I would love to,' she said.

As her eyes took me in, I picked up my lingerie and slowly pulled the pieces back onto my naked body. Even as I gave her one last private show, her eyes remained on my face, not my body. It sent a thrill through me.

As I stood, finally clasping my bra on, I spoke without thinking.

'You're bad news.' Instantly regretting my words, I waited for her to be irritated by my statement, but instead, she laughed and her smile was captivating.

Walking past me to leave the room, she looked back one last time.

'Take care of yourself.' In that moment, it felt like she truly cared and wanted me to be okay. It was a weird sensation but it made me feel safe. I didn't quite understand it myself; it was a foreign feeling.

As she faded into the crowd once more, I found my eyes searching for her the rest of the night, but I didn't see her again. When I went home I found myself thinking about her as I shut my eyes and went to bed.

# 3
# VALENTINA

It had been a few days since Matt's bucks party and I still couldn't shake the thoughts of Sunshine that were plaguing me. She consumed my mind and even found her way into my dreams. She was magnetic and those eyes were the sexiest thing I had ever seen. I was infatuated and I felt like a horny teenager obsessing over her first crush, not the twenty-five-year-old that I was.

Matt's words rattled around in my mind as I replayed every minute of that night over and over again. When I caught up with him following our shared dance, he told me he'd felt like he was interrupting something between us and that he should have left us alone for that dance. He swore that, although it was her job to make her clients feel wanted, he thought she genuinely wanted me. The palpable chemistry between us being clear for all to see.

It was comforting, in a sense, to know that he had seen what I'd felt—that I wasn't completely delusional, even though that was exactly how I felt, having already fantasised a million different ways I might run into her again. I felt obsessed, and some of those fantasies had me feeling like a stalker. I suppose the apple truly didn't fall far from the tree, knowing my family's proclivities—well, Zane's at least.

Tonight, was not the night to lose myself to my all-consuming thoughts. I had to be sharp. This dinner had been on the books for the last month. Xavier, my eldest brother, ran the family and our organisation, which meant he was the one who arranged these dreadfully boring dinners each month. I had already established that I had no interest in joining the more sinister business enterprises we owned and operated, but I still had value to give when it came to propelling us and our objectives forward.

My hand in marriage was highly sought after; many families and foreign criminal organisations sought a foothold in our city and saw allying through marriage as the perfect opportunity given my family ran almost everything. I was not opposed to the idea myself; I had always assumed this would be my reality, and my brothers had promised I would have a say in the final match. I didn't have a strong inclination myself towards finding love, so something arranged always seemed more convenient. That's precisely what these dinners have been about over the last eight months.

Tonight, we were sitting down with Alexei Petrov, the first in line to the Russian *bratva* currently run by his father.

I sat at the head of the table in our formal dining room. In any other family or household, that seat would have belonged to Xavier when there were guests, but here it was mine. My brothers always taught me I wasn't secondary to any man, not even them. They would not accept someone in my life who wanted to push me down, forcing me to live a meek, subservient life. For one it did not suit me and if we were truly being honest I would kill anyone that tried.

What no one outside our family knew was that I was the second best fighter of my siblings, with only Zane outmatching me due to his sheer size, strength and penchant for violence. Xavier was the brains of the organisation and had a quiet power to him, whereas I had speed and agility, as well as a strategic mind. Even though I didn't have an active role in the family, they respected me as an equal—but they preferred me to be safe and outside of the immediate fray. I would always be their little sister, no matter my age. The girl they had fought so hard to protect when the world wanted to tear us to shreds as children, with no one and nothing to our names.

Xavier stalked into the room and took a seat on my left. Even while seated, you could easily see how tall he was. My brother was handsome and always composed, wearing suits and carrying himself with perfect posture, but there was an edge to him that simmered under the surface. You could catch glimpses of it in his almost black eyes that matched his hair.

Zane followed behind him, taking the seat next to Xav. Where Xav was tall and lean, Zane was built like a beast; he oozed demonic energy, which completely went against his softer, personality when he spoke to those he cared about. He had a wicked sense of humour that not many knew how to process, especially since Z was known as one of the best enforcers in the business. He had the highest kill count in the country, and he was truly feared for his torture techniques. It was not uncommon for people to opt to end their own lives rather than face him and his depraved ways. The man was truly a psychopath in every sense of the word, but to me, he was just Z, my big brother.

'How are you feeling, V? If tonight's a success I keep a

stash of condoms in the cloak room, just grab some on your way out.'

'Really, Z?! Can we not speak about V having sex? It's really not very funny,' Xav snapped at Z's crass comments. Always poking at our stoic leader.

Before we could continue, the formal dining room doors opened as Evelyn, our housekeeper, ushered in Alexei. His eyes briefly glanced in the direction of my brothers as he sent a polite nod their way. His eyes raked over my body, taking me in before he briefly paused to assess the seating arrangement. He hesitated before making his way to the empty seat on my right. Refusing to give an inch—knowing the power play had already commenced—I remained seated as he came to my side, lifting my hand as he placed a chaste kiss on it before taking his seat.

I could feel Xav's muscles physically tighten at the display of affection, while Z's eyes twinkled with amusement. Z wanted to watch the world burn and tonight would be a slice of that.

Alexei spent the next ten minutes speaking to Xav about business and the future of the bratva until Evelyn walked in with the entrées. So far, the food had been the most captivating part of the night. Without waiting, I helped myself to the steak tartare. Alexei raised an eyebrow at my audacity to start before a guest. I quickly realised that this would never work between us because I had no energy for false pretences and showmanship.

He seemed undeterred as he finally focused his efforts on wooing me instead of my brother, understanding that I had the power to decide whether this would proceed, not them, as they continued to deflect his questions back to me for an answer.

'Tell me about yourself, Valentina. I hear that you love

to read. What are you currently reading?' he asked innocently enough, seeming to at least be faking his interest to fool most people, but not me. He didn't care about me—only the De Luca name and what it could afford him, just like the rest.

'Oh, you wouldn't know it.' I brushed off his question, not wanting to engage. I wished he would just redirect his attention back to my brothers.

'I'm quite well read; I might surprise you,' he said, leaning in.

I set my fork down and leaned back in my chair, crossing my arms.

'It's called *Whore for Your Bloodlust*. It's about a young woman who captures the attention of a serial killer, but instead of fearing him, she feels wanted. So, she wants to do everything she can to prove herself to him. Right now, I'm reading quite a poignant scene where she gives him a blow job after watching him murder a man in cold blood. The author has quite a way with words. I can almost feel the stickiness of the victim's blood in my own hair as he grips the back of her head, forcing her to choke on his enormous—'

'What the fuck, V?!' Xav boomed as Z broke out in fits of laughter knowing I had stolen the book from his collection.

I didn't react; instead, I watched as Alexei's face slightly paled. Not because he was squeamish; you couldn't afford to be in his family's line of work. It was disgust I saw written on his face, but I never quite understood the word 'shame'.

Wanting to push him further, I leaned forward, entering his space. 'I have a lot of fantasies like those, think you could keep up with me?' I left Alexei speechless and Xav with a throbbing headache as he pinched the bridge of his nose, shaking his head and trying his best not to lose it in front of company.

'Liar, we all know you're the vanilla one in the family, you little sundae,' Z remarked with a smirk on his face. He wasn't wrong. I liked to read these stories, but what I actually craved in all of them wasn't the physicality; it was the earth-shattering love, longing and possessiveness. I wanted to be consumed and I wanted to consume. Without meaning to, my mind went back to Sunshine and her eyes. That was the closest I had ever felt to touching that feeling. Realising this, I stood ready to leave.

'Sorry, Alexei, I don't quite see this working out. You need someone young, impressionable that you can turn into your perfect little trad wife, but that won't ever be me. I know my power and I get the sense that you like to be the one in control.'

Then, turning to Z, I motioned for him to stand. 'I need to go to the Velvet Room. Take me?'

Curiosity got the best of him as he turned to lead the way, leaving Xav muttering curses under his breath.

When we arrived at my brother's club, he opened the door for me. One thing I loved about Z was that he never asked questions; he preferred to observe a situation—unless he had a knife to a man's throat and his job was quite *literally* to ask questions in the most brutal way possible. To Z, this was all one big amusing play, and he wanted to see why I had demanded to come here of all places, seeing as I had never had an interest before.

'You have someone working for you—Sunshine. Where is she?' I asked as I pulled up a stool at the bar.

Z went behind it to pour me a drink, making my favourite: gin and tonic with lime.

'I was expecting one of the bartenders to have piqued

your interest, not one of my girls. Interesting... It's nearly 8:00 pm, so she's likely in the staff lounge getting ready for her shift. She starts soon.'

I turned in my chair, ready to make my way to the lounge. I needed to see her again.

'No. That is a safe space for the women; no one enters that space save for them, not even me. Do not take that from them. Sit and wait.'

Giving a frustrated sigh, I sat back down; he was right.

'V, I'll say this once and only once. You think we come from trauma? You've got nothing on her. Hurt her and I hurt you. I know you're blood, but I swore an oath to protect each one of these women and I will not let you make me a liar. Do not go anywhere near her if you aren't serious about her.' He knocked back an entire glass of whiskey like it was water. The man loved pain.

'I don't know what I am, Zane. That's why I need to see her again—to figure out what this is.' I felt guilty and selfish because if what he said was true, then he was also right, and I should stay far away. But I doubted I could do that anymore, as she had continued to plague my mind these last few days. There was an undeniable pull that I didn't want to resist anymore.

'Well, figure it out quickly and no games. She's not an experiment for you or an act of rebellion. You know Xav would never force a marriage you didn't want, but I can run interference when it comes to next month's dinner. You have one month to figure it out; by then, a decision needs to be made for everyone's sake. I must say though, this makes a lot of sense to me.'

'What does?' I questioned, thrown off by his last comment.

'You've always loved to care for those who are damaged.

I also can't picture you ever submitting to any man. I kind of thought you would have explored this side of yourself when you were younger, but better late than never.' I was completely shocked by his declaration.

'Your lady's here, so what are you gonna do?' he asked, nodding his head towards the main stage.

Pushing off the stool, I didn't look back.

# 4
# SUNSHINE

It was my first night on the main stage. I had been working hard on this show for the last couple of weeks. The audition process was grueling and only the best girls secured a slot up here. They were always themed, for some reason. Tiny costumes got the clients off, so I centered my performance around a bored 1920s housewife. At least that's how I had sold it to management; it was really a homage to my favourite portrait painter, Giovanni Boldini, who had a way of painting women in such a sensual and feminine manner with his swirling brush strokes.

The lights were dim as I stepped onto the stage, covered in a vintage dress that looked like it had walked off the set of *Bridgerton*, but would inevitably become skimpier and skimpier until I was completely bare before the audience. I had wondered for a long time if there was something wrong with me for finding comfort and power in this line of work after everything I had gone through. However, it wasn't until I started seeing one of the onsite counsellors across the road, despite opting to stay in my own apartment downtown, that I truly understood why. It was because I never processed my trauma that, as an adult, I reenacted it to gain some semblance or illusion of control. I was stuck in an unconscious cycle of revictimisation, but I wasn't quite ready to pull myself out of it yet. I still needed this. I'd spent so long viewing myself in a particular way, living in shame and confusion. Stepping out of that was terrifying, but these moments were when I felt peace, when things made sense and when I held all the control.

The music transformed into the melodic and sultry tune I had chosen as the lights slowly came back on in time with the crescendo of the song. I raised my head, looking at the end of the stage as I walked forward, swaying my hips and dragging my feather duster against me, but then I saw her. I stumbled briefly, missing my cue as I stood still, completely struck. My mystery girl was back; not only that, but she was sitting at the end of the stage, front and centre, watching me with a devious smirk on her lips and hunger in her eyes.

Taking a deep breath, I forced myself to keep moving and dancing, engaging with the crowd. But, for some reason, I was too scared to approach her the way I did the others who lined the stage. My eyes kept drifting to her though, more times than they should have. My heart wasn't in this dance, as my mind was consumed by thoughts of her trying to figure out what she was doing here. I hoped she was here for me but that was a naive thought. Every time our gazes met, I saw the slight tug of her lips. She liked it when I looked at her while I danced for the others.

It wasn't long until my set came to a close. I stood at the end of the stage, breathless, as I posed while the lights faded to black. Mystery girl stood and nodded towards the back, as if asking me to meet her there. Was I perhaps reading far too much into this, or was that, in fact, an invitation? There was only one way to find out.

I hurried off the stage, changed in our employee lounge and then headed back onto the floor. I had to decline a few propositions and requests for private dances as I walked through the throng of people; there was only one person I wanted to dance for tonight.

Just before the entrance to the back private rooms, I found her leaning against the wall, arms crossed, looking almost bored in all black. She wore badarse leather lace-up boots, skintight jeans and a mesh long-sleeved crop top. Joining her, I leaned on the wall next to her, taking in her long brown hair and sharp features.

'What are you looking at?' I asked, turning my body so that my breasts just grazed her crossed arms. She was a vision. Slowly, she turned her body towards me, raking her eyes over my body, from my toes, over my purple lace underwear and up my body.

'Nothing, I was just waiting,' she said in the most delicious tone.

'Waiting for what?' I asked, hoping the answer would be me.

'My little ray of sunshine,' she said, uncrossing her arms as she reached for my hand. My heart stuttered as a grin escaped me without warning.

'Care for a dance?' I asked, pulling on her hand as I pushed off the wall and led her to the back rooms. I took her silence as she followed obediently as a *yes*.

I found the most secluded room down two halls. It was strictly reserved for our VIP clients who booked at least an hour session, but tonight was slow, and no one would mind I was occupying it for a single dance.

I watched her eyes take in the details of the room. On the far wall was a wide couch that could honestly double as a bed; there was a pole in the corner and a large TV on the wall beside us. The walls were a crushed red velvet. It was a bit on the nose, considering the name of the club, but I did like the feel of it and the atmosphere it created.

'What do you want?' I inquired as I pushed her down onto the couch and circled to a stop in front of her.

'You. All night,' she breathed as she rested back onto her elbows, taking me in. I felt powerful.

'Our longest dance is an hour. If you're looking for someone for all night, I can find one of the girls from upstairs to come get you,' I tested. I wanted her—God, how I wanted her—but I wasn't about to lose the only good job I had ever had by giving in to my baser instincts. Besides, I wanted to see what she would do with the option. If this was purely physical. Because for me, it insanely already felt deeper.

'I'm not interested in anyone else or what goes on upstairs. I'll take a dance, though. Do your worst,' she challenged.

So that's what I did. Moving in time with the rhythm of the music. Like last time, she didn't spare a glance at my body; instead, she stared right into my soul and shredded me to pieces. I became a ball of want and need as I danced against her body, breathed in her sweet tobacco-tinged scent and touched her bare skin. Once I had pulled off the last of my lace, she sat up straighter, eyes raking over the curves and planes of my body, drinking me in. But her eyes didn't linger where the others did. Instead, she took in the planes of my skin—the dips and the grooves. Not the tantalising things on full display.

Raising her fingers, she placed the tips of her nails on the outside of my thigh, dragging them ever so slowly up and over my hip. I stilled, forgetting about the dance and tuning out the music as my breath became shallow, panting with each inch of skin she set alight. She dragged her nails over my stomach and up my sternum, between my breasts, until her fingers curled around my throat. She pulled me close until we were just a breath away. If I only moved forward slightly, our lips would touch. But instead, she held me in place, staring at them as she bit down on her own. I couldn't help licking mine as I salivated, wanting to taste her. The movement set her eyes ablaze with desire. Her fingers clenched my throat tighter, but instead of that familiar fear, it sent a rush through me. There was no pain, just pleasure. I was in control of every moment of this game, and we both knew it.

Her left hand woke me from my trance as it trailed up the inside of my other thigh— slowly, ever so slowly—as my insides churned with need. I couldn't stop myself from squirming. I wanted to rub my thighs together and scratch this infernal need that was building and that I wouldn't be able to sate. She paused right before she met my opening; my breathing had got ragged but so was hers. At least she wasn't completely unaffected as she drove me further towards insanity.

Without warning, she gripped the inside of my thigh tightly, as her body shuddered. She was on the cusp of losing her own tenuous thread of control and something in me wanted to push her further.

Leaning forward, I whispered a moan into her ear, letting her know just what she was doing to me. As her grip tightened on me, I spread my fingers into her hair then pulled, bringing her closer to me as our bodies collided, no longer hovering in this unspoken threshold that couldn't be crossed. As I clung to her and as she held me, her left hand now moving to the small of my back pushing me further into her as our bodies moved as one, we ground on each other. I moved each of my legs on either side of her thigh and knowing exactly what I needed, she moved her thigh against me. She held it there, allowing me to take control of my own pleasure.

I moved up and down her thigh, harder and faster as I gasped for breath. Her hand let go of my throat and wound to the back of my hair as she pulled my head back, wanting to see my face; instead, I pulled her closer, burying her face in my breasts. I needed to feel her against every inch of my body, since I couldn't have her inside me, and I chased my pleasure against her leg. My body wound tighter as I pulled her back and sunk my teeth into her shoulder. My breath left my lungs and I crashed over the precipice of biting through my orgasm and the scream I wanted to release.

We sat like that for a few moments as we caught our breath and the ringing in my ears faded.

'I think I'm in lust with you,' I breathed, not comprehending what I had just done. I had broken so many rules but right now I didn't care.

'I can tell. So much for biting being against the rules.' She chuckled.

'Oh my God, I am so sorry!' I stammered, reality hitting me in waves; I had just crossed so many lines and without her consent. What was wrong with me?! I stood, reaching for my lingerie, ready to bolt in humiliation.

'Where do you think you're going?' she asked as she gripped my wrist, pulling me onto the couch beside her.

'I wasn't complaining, Sunshine. I'm pretty sure I'm in love with you,' she said so certainly, and sure, it almost made me believe her. But I had heard those words from clients before as they got swept up in the moment. This was the first time I had been as equally swept up and wanted her to feel how I felt. Hope was a dangerous thing, though, and only led to disappointment and pain.

'I should get back out onto the floor,' I stammered, picking up my purple lace and fleeing without even putting them back on.

'Scared? I didn't peg you for the type,' she called after me. But she was dead wrong; I wasn't scared. I knew what it was to feel real terror, and this was a touch of embarrassment and nervousness at best. There was only one man I feared, and it's why I had taken a job under Zane and the De Luca family. I had heard the rumours of how he had created this safe haven, how he protected his girls and how he was the only man in the country who instilled blood curdling fear in everyone he came across. No one dared to cross him or the people who worked for him unless they were asking to die.

No, what I felt now was disappointment in myself for wanting something, or someone. Least of all, someone I barely knew. I just couldn't. My feelings had fooled me before, and they had nearly broken me in the most literal sense of the word.

# 5
# VALENTINA

Sunshine using my leg to get off was by far the hottest fucking thing I had ever experienced. I spent three days thinking about it. Zane had refused to give me her contact information, which I respected, but I was begrudgingly annoyed about it. Apparently, she only worked weekends; I found that out from one of the bartenders that night after she had run off like a deer in headlights.

Today, however, was a day filled with distractions. I wouldn't have the time to even spare a thought for the endearing minx who made me feel things I hadn't felt with anyone before, man or woman.

It took a long six months to settle the paperwork for this space, but thanks to my dear brother Xavier and the weight our family name holds, I finally landed the gallery of my dreams. It lay in the centre of the art precinct. As a child I had snuck in here to stare at all of the incredible works of art and dreamed of the day I would hold my own show featuring my own pieces. Now the day was here.

It smelled of fresh paint, and I could taste the bitterness of newly polished concrete in the air. The last month had been a whirlwind of renovations. It felt expansive yet warm in this space, with mood lighting cast in every direction from the hundreds of lights lining the industrial ceiling. Right now, it was empty, but I planned to fill it soon enough with parts of my soul.

My heels echoed in the space as I walked to the side and down a hidden hallway. My legs burned from walking the two flights of stairs to get to my studio above the gallery. This room was equally large, but where the ground level was barren, this was overwhelming chaos.

I had multiple shelves, tables, and boxes overflowing with supplies. Streaks of sunlight warmed me to my bones as I walked by the windows that lined each wall, checking on the progress of all my work. The smell of oil paintings made me feel at home; the rough, jagged edges of my sculptures under my fingers called for the work that still needed to be done, and the smooth surfaces of my ceramics had me eager to glaze them.

Many artists seemed to only dabble in one medium of art, but I had a short attention span, and everything fascinated me. It helped to oscillate between my pieces when I got stuck and that's exactly where I found myself now. Stuck.

Years I had spent dreaming of this gallery and my first show, and as I looked at all my work before me, none of it felt right. There was a disconnect between the girl who had started these pieces and the woman I had become. There was no clear theme or message. It was a collection of my trials and errors in trying new things, flexing my skills without any cohesion. This was not an exhibit; it was a mess.

I wasn't allowed to go home until I figured out what my show would be about. This self-imposed sanction was the only way I could move forward with this dream of mine. I was paralysed with indecision and imposter syndrome, and I had been for some time now. Ever since I signed that contract, my drive to create had vanished along with the eleven million in my bank account that I paid for this space.

The only way for me to move past a creative block was to sit down and force myself to paint. I let my emotions, the colours and brushstrokes, pull out what it needed from me, without thought or worry. I painted just to paint.

Three hours had passed, and as I stepped away from the canvas to take in my work, I instantly realised what was staring back at me—or rather, *who*.

It was my little ray of sunshine. Unknowingly, my mind had drifted to thoughts of her; my brush followed every plane of her body that my fingers had touched. Not thinking too much of it, I went to look for the perfect red that matched the lingerie she had worn that first night I saw her. After forty-five minutes of emptying every drawer, box, and shelf of my paints, I was at a loss. Luckily, there was an art supply store at the end of the street that I had yet to check out.

The art store was almost cozy with its wooden floors and shelves. It was rich with supplies but I quickly noticed they only had the most high-quality brands in stock. This was an art store for true artists. Not those that crafted things on the weekend as a hobby. Walking through the first room that contained different types of paper, pastels and pencils, I moved towards the back room where the shelves were filled with brushes and paints. I stared at the options, almost at a loss; the decision of what shade of red to choose seemed to paralyse me. It had to be perfect. She was perfect.

Lost in my thoughts, I didn't notice the sales assistant

walking up behind me. She asked me something, but my mind was singularly focused. Something light tapped my shoulder, pulling me from my reverie.

'Excuse me, is there something I can help you with?' a voice asked as she picked up the red paint I had been staring at, passing it to me.

'Sunshine,' I breathed. Her spine went rigid as her eyes snapped to mine, finally realising who I was. She looked different when clothed. Her hair was braided now, unlike her bouncy coils from last time. Her makeup was simpler, and her eyes were hidden behind her thick framed reading glasses. I wanted to pull them off and see those eyes without any barriers. It took her a moment to compose herself and push all the shock from her features. She tucked a stray hair behind her ear that didn't exist as she drew her shoulders back.

'Y-you're painting a sunset scape then? This red would be perfect. Would you like me to ring you up?' she stuttered, fumbling over her words, trying to brush past this moment.

Zeroing in, her name tag screamed at me. '*Namazzi*.' It rolled off my tongue beautifully. Her body shivered at my use of her name. Without waiting, she took the red paint and strode towards the register.

'You're an artist?' She didn't meet my eyes as she spoke, a tinge of a blush shading her cheeks.

'Trying to be.' That got a reaction; her eyes snapped up to meet mine, looking at me curiously. I wanted to ask; I knew who she was, and I could tell she recognised me, but this was her job. I couldn't; I could. I shouldn't; I should. Losing my internal battle, the next words left my lips without restraint.

'Sunshine, are you working tonight?' Her eyes widened before she cast them down and shook her head in shame.

The feel of her skin as I lifted her chin and her mind from her shame sent fire through my veins.

'What time do you get off?' I asked, still holding her face as my fingers slid to her cheek, my thumb caressing her jaw. She sucked in a breath and bit down hard on her bottom lip. She was waging her own internal war, but I wouldn't let her hurt herself. My thumb brushed over her bottom lip pulling it slightly, telling her to release it. I dragged it over the indentations her teeth made, soothing the pain, and I repeated the question.

'At six,' she said softly, barely above a whisper, entranced by the strokes of my thumb.

'I'll be waiting outside at six,' I said, tapping my card as I drew my hand back and walked away with my paint in hand. If I had stayed there for one moment longer, I would have lost myself.

I couldn't believe she worked here, so close to my studio and gallery. This was divine intervention, if I had ever seen it. Z had all her records and would have known she worked near me, but he didn't even hint that I should buy new supplies. Irritation flared, though I understood why he had done it. He protected them—all of them.

The rest of my day had been a blur of pacing around my studio, filled with so much energy that there was no way I could pick up my brush again. Not being able to control myself or quiet my nerves, I found myself in front of the art supply shop, smoking a cigarette one hour early. I watched the pedestrians filter by as I continued smoking through every cigarette in my pack, the nerves building. One man curiously circled the block three times, trying to get his steps in while wearing head to toe athletic gear that didn't quite fit in with his casual stroll. By the time I noticed my girl—yes, mine—closing up the shop, I was standing next to a pile of cigarette butts. Pushing off the wall, I met her as she turned to scan the street for me.

'What do you prefer to be called?' I asked, catching her by surprise. She hesitated, looking down at her name tag, biting the inside of her cheek, before casting me that brilliant smile that warmed me to my bones.

'Namazzi... but you, I like the way you call me Sunshine.' She blushed.

'My little ray of Sunshine it is.' Her blush deepened, and it made me want to bite her bottom lip until it matched the shade of red on her cheeks.

'I still don't know yours.'

'You can call me V; all my friends do.' Not wanting to share my actual name in case it triggered her to make the connection between me and her boss. Though Xav and I looked like siblings, Z took mostly after our father in terms of sheer size.

She tested the taste of my name on her tongue. 'V, I like that.'

My core clenched as she bit down on that bottom lip again. Surely, this would be the thing that drove me to insanity.

I hadn't quite planned what we were going to do; I had just wanted to see her. Instead, we found ourselves ambling through the streets in silence while she stole glances at me until her stomach audibly rumbled.

'Hungry, Sunshine?'

She nodded, but her nerves got the best of her, preventing her from speaking. I placed a comforting hand in hers, and the feel of her shocked flinch, followed by the gentle squeeze as she settled into the comfort, had my heart singing.

I could have taken her anywhere; our family had

numerous restaurants. Instead, I took her to a hole in the wall that my brothers and I frequented while growing up. It was in a rougher part of town, so I pulled her to my side as my hand slid around her waist. She melted into me but didn't seem to mind the neighbourhood.

Guido's was an old Italian-style restaurant, complete with worn out vinyl flooring and fluorescent lights that had me squinting my eyes, but it was my safe space for much of my childhood. Guido came barrelling out of the kitchen the moment he saw me.

'My beautiful Val, what are you doing here darling? You should have told me you were coming. How are the boys? Are they coming?' he asked, squeezing me in a warm embrace, almost lifting me from the floor. He was an older, large man with a potbelly and greying hair, but he was strong. He had left a similar life to the one my family found ourselves in to open this restaurant. We had tried to set him up with a new restaurant or expand to new locations, but this was his little slice of humble heaven, and he enjoyed it here.

'They're good, Papa G. I didn't know I was coming either; my friend here was hungry, and without thinking, I walked home.' I smiled.

Ushering us to a table by the window, he sat us down and loaded it with bread. Still water for myself and sparkling for Sunshine. I had always hated the bitter taste of it.

'Is that your father?' Sunshine asked.

'In every way that matters. My older brothers and I grew up without any family in a group home not far from here. We would sneak off to Guido's and he would feed us; he gave us our first jobs and sometimes let us sleep upstairs when things got... rough.'

'Oh, I had no idea, I'm sorry,' she said, fidgeting with the sleeve of her top.

'Hey now, there's nothing to be sorry for. It's life; it just was, and it just is. It's not painful; it never was. I was surrounded by love thanks to Papa G and my brothers,' I said, grasping her hand over the table.

'Now tell me about you,' I probed. Her eyes doubled in size with a flash of panic before she settled it and flashed her signature smile; but for the first time, I saw a small part of it falter behind some pain.

'Not much to say. Ran away at sixteen. Found myself couch surfing for a while, then I was sleeping on the streets. Once I was eighteen, I found that dancing was one of the few professions that didn't care if you completed high school or had a permanent address. Slowly, I worked, found a place to stay, and then, after a while, I found myself at the Velvet Room.'

'Why'd you run?' I asked.

'You know how it is; Mum got a new boyfriend and he couldn't keep his hands to himself. She blamed me, of course. Said I seduced him. Joke's on me because look at what I'm doing for a living now.' She laughed bitterly.

Her hand was soft in mine as I squeezed it in comfort.

'There is nothing wrong with what you're doing. It's not the only thing you're doing, though, is it? Why the art supply store? You must make enough at my— the Velvet Room.'

Rolling her shoulders back and levelling me with a stare that challenged me to I don't know what, she said, 'I want to be a gallery director. I never thought I could be one... not until I started working for Zane De Luca.' She whispered my brother's name. 'I know you've probably heard the rumours, and as terrifying as he is, he's so supportive of us.

He's paying for me to take a course at the local art college and got me the job at the art supply store. He said it was a great way to meet local artists and network.' Looking me up and down she finished, 'He was right.'

'If I can be an artist, you can be a gallery director.' Then her smile became wholly genuine, and it took the air right out of my lungs.

The rest of the evening was spent talking about everything and anything but not once did I let go of her hand as we ate. I wanted to know every little thing about her, and with every bit of information I learned, I fell slightly deeper into the hold she already had over me. Eventually, she began to yawn, and I knew I needed to get her home.

Outside the restaurant, my car was parked. As I fished out a set of keys and unlocked it, I opened the door for her, but she stared at me in confusion.

'How? We walked here? Also, what the fuck is this? I thought you were a struggling artist?' she exclaimed, waving an arm at my two-million-dollar Aston Martin Valour.

'I never said I was struggling. You heard orphan and assumed that meant poor. As for how, I had a friend drop off the car and give my keys to Papa G while we were eating.' I smirked, enjoying the slight crease of confusion that marked the space between her brows; she seemed embarrassed by her assumption of me.

'I-I'm sorry,' she stammered, cheeks flaming.

'If you want to make it up to me, let me drive you home, Sunshine.'

'I don't live far from here; I can walk,' she said, shrinking away from the car. That explained why she hadn't been uncomfortable walking through this side of town at this time of night.

'Get in, Namazzi. I want to drive you home and you're going to let me. Please,' I added, to sweeten the demand. She hesitated still.

'Why? Why did you take me out tonight?' she asked, confused but taking the barest step forward.

'Why did you rub yourself against me until you came?' I asked, pressing in closer to her until my body crowded her and I was all but purring the words against her ear.

'Tell me, Sunshine, can you truly deny this pull between us? It's cosmic, divinely inspired and wholly earth shattering. I have never craved a person the way I crave you. Not your body, but the mind behind those mesmerising eyes. I want to know you and seep into every fibre of your being, just as you have seeped into my mind, body and soul, utterly consuming me. I don't think I'll ever feel whole again without you in my life. The moment my eyes saw your smile, you became my north star. This, my sweet darling, is fate. Tell me I'm wrong.' I bit down lightly on her earlobe and dragged my teeth down as her body vibrated beneath me, a soft moan escaping her lips and echoing in my mind.

Something snapped within her, whether it was my words or my touch, I found myself being slammed against my car as her leg hiked up and wrapped around my hip, her lips crashing into mine, hungry, consuming. Her tongue was warm and eager, dancing with my own in a game of push and pull. Sparks trailed across my skin, her frantic fingers touching everywhere, grasping for a hold on reality as she descended into desire.

It could have been minutes or hours; I lost all sense of time. But when we finally pulled apart, gasping for air, one thing was certain. She was mine, and the stare that met me told me I was hers.

After that, she was compliant and let me drive her home; it was a ten-minute drive from the restaurant but I wished it were longer. She lived in an old, red brick apartment building. My gods, I wanted to follow her, but instead, I let her go, giving her my number and leaving her with the power to decide where this would go from here. I was all in.

# 6
# SUNSHINE

I waited all of five minutes before texting V after she dropped me off. My hands were still shaking with the adrenaline from that kiss and the way she gripped my thigh as she sped through the streets at night. I was dripping with need now as I laid in bed, rubbing my thighs together, while I typed out the perfect message, then deleted it, and retyped it again and again, finally settling on something completely unoriginal.

Sunshine: Thanks for tonight V.

Was my message pathetic? Yes. But nothing I could say was good enough, and my mind was a turbulent ocean right now, with crashing waves of confusion. It took thirty minutes for V to get home and reply to me.

V: I should be thanking you Sunshine. How are you feeling about my declarations? I know how your body felt, but I want to know how your mind is feeling about us.

*Us.* It was beautiful—terrifyingly beautiful. Everyone I had ever been with always said "mine", never "us", and I loved it coming from V. Could I trust it? I wanted to. I wanted to free fall into whatever this was and have no cares. To be swept away, leaving my past dead and buried, but that's not how my life had ever worked—especially not since I realised tonight that we came from very different worlds. We may have both started from humble, if not traumatic, beginnings, but I was still stuck in that world, whereas V looked like she owned it and more.

Sunshine: It may be too early to start talking about us. You barely know me. I barely know you and if I'm being honest I'm slightly intimidated after tonight. We live in two very different worlds, V. I don't see how this works. Is there a connection? Yes. Do you make me feel things I never have before? Yes. Do I want you? Yes. But life isn't that simple, my life is anything but simple and you seem to have it good right now. I don't want to drag you down to my level when you've transcended it already.

I fought sleep while waiting for her reply, but it seemed I had scared her off; soon, the heaviness of my eyes won out. This was for the best.

In the morning when I woke, there was still no response from V. It was a good thing, but some twisted part of me unfairly felt disappointed. I tried not to overthink my message and to avoid flinging myself against a wall due to the self-doubt and embarrassment that were itching at my skin.

A small part of me hoped I would see her at the shop again today, that she would need another brush or some paint. My contradictory feelings were making my head swim but I didn't bother rationalising it.

I was slower getting ready, constantly checking my phone, but when I stepped outside my apartment to catch the bus, there she was. Leaning against her car in the cool morning air, smoking her cigarette between leather-gloved fingers.

I stood there staring at her for a few minutes, not quite understanding what was happening. Had I not sent that message last night? Was it all just some sick dream?

Her piercing gaze held mine, watching and waiting. Allowing me to take my time.

'Jump in, I'll give you a ride to work,' she said, holding the door open as her shoe crushed the cigarette butt into the pavement when I approached.

'Why are you here?' I stammered, stepping forward but refusing to get into the car. 'You didn't even respond to my message last night.' The moment I said the words, I wanted to take them back; they even sounded desperate and grating on my nerves. She owed me nothing.

'I thought that conversation was better had in person. Let's talk in the car, where it's warm, Sunshine.'

I hesitated once more, but the way she said my name melted me a little. She said it with reverence. V pointed to a steaming hot cup of coffee sitting in the cup holder, waiting for me.

Her heated leather seats wrapped me up in a warm hug that set my nerves at ease.

'Sunshine, I want to make this clear. I have no fucking idea what we are doing. I don't know where it's going or how it will work. What I do know is I want to explore this, I want to know you and my God, I want to fuck you. So fuck every excuse you can think of for us not to work. There are a million more reasons we will. As for your concerns about us living in different worlds, they're unfounded. I live in the same reality you do. We may live a little differently, but that doesn't mean we can't live this life together. What are you so scared of? Tell me. Because I won't leave you alone for reasons as flimsy as those.'

I didn't even realise I was smiling until her thumb traced my jaw, pulling me in and holding me until we were just millimeters apart from each other's lips. I breathed in her scent, tinged with jasmine tea and the double shot long black she had been drinking, mixed with the dark aroma of tobacco.

'Tell me,' she whispered, holding my jaw in place so I couldn't push forward, leaning into that kiss I so desperately wanted to feel again. It took a moment to unscramble my brain and remember what she had asked.

'I can't be hurt again. My ex, he hurt me. He broke me, and the moment he finds out I may be happy with someone, he'll hurt you. I can't be with anyone, not seriously, anyway. I can't risk his wrath again.'

'Oh, sweet girl, a man acting like a petulant child and treating people like toys is not something I have ever feared. You don't know this about me yet, but there is no safer place for you than by my side. I think it's time you met my brothers.' She smirked, radiating a confidence that made me relax a little.

'Don't you think that's a bit rushed? I don't even know your real name.'

'It's Valentina, sweet girl, but you can call me whatever you please. Anything that comes out of those lips will be my favourite thing to be called.' Leaning into me, she kissed me deeply, slowly, exploring the corners of my mouth. My concerns faded—that was what I had felt from the first moment I was in her presence; it was peace, it was safety and I was desperate for it.

'There's that smile again,' she breathed against my lips. 'Let's get you to work.'

This car ride felt more comfortable than the last, but instead of relaxing I was overwhelmed with need as V's fingers made their way up my thigh, searing my skin. I wore skinny jeans, and I could feel everything as though my legs were bare. This time she drew her fingers higher, grazing her knuckles over my slit. I sucked in a breath which drew V's gaze to mine. She had a wicked grin and her eyes were aflame with a desire that I'm sure matched my own.

'Tell me what you want.' Her voice caressed my ears as her fingers lightly trailed over me.

'You. I want you,' I breathed, struggling for control until she pulled back slightly. Our surroundings faded back into light, and we were sitting out front the art supply store. 'Fuck!' I huffed, slamming the back of my head against the seat and closing my eyes, trying to calm my mind. I had work. V laughed at my frustration and that sound was entrancing.

'When will I see you next?' I asked. I was falling—hard and fast—and I wanted to spend more time with her. I was infatuated with this woman, and minute by minute, I stopped caring about the things that had held me back with her. I wanted something good in my life, and my God, was she a slice of heaven.

'Tonight. I'll pick you up at the end of your shift. Now go, before I lose my grip on the little restraint I have to let you go.' It did things to me, to know I wasn't the only one so affected right now.

Kissing her on the cheek and flashing her a smile, I left, stealing one last glance as I stepped into the store. She didn't leave until I was safely inside. That gesture alone gave me hope. I felt safe, which was something rare for me.

A folded piece of paper lay on the floor as though it had been slid under there. Picking it up, I placed it next to the register to give to the owner.

The day was a blur, I kept thinking about the feel of V's tongue, lips and fingers on me. I wanted to feel more. I decided tonight that I would, so when she picked me up, I bounced over to her, leaned against her car, and flung my arms around her, kissing her cheek. I would no longer be afraid to grab hold of what I wanted. I had done that for so long that I was tired of it. I hadn't heard from Jason in months. Surely he had moved on after Z threatened him at the club when I first started. Even Jason wasn't stupid enough to cross my new boss.

V wasn't surprised by my sudden change in demeanor; instead, her arms wrapped around my waist, pulling me in closer as she nuzzled into my neck, breathing in the scent of me.

'V, can we grab some takeaway and go back to mine? Maybe snuggle up and watch a movie?' I asked coyly.

V nodded but laughed, knowing there would likely not be much eating of food or movie-watching given the way I was plastered against her body, all but grinding on her. She never felt close enough. I needed her under my skin and inside of me.

My apartment was a rundown shoebox, probably nothing like the luxury she lived in given the price of her car. But she had started where I had been, so I knew there was no judgement as she took in the mismatched furniture, most of which I had bought from garage sales or found on the street and cleaned up. It was a small studio where everything, except for the bathroom, was in one big room. The only saving grace were the high ceilings and large windows behind my bed.

She placed our pizzas on the table and went to the kitchen, rummaging for plates and cups while I got changed. My body buzzed with anticipation, so when I walked back in wearing my PJs, instead of taking the seat next to hers, I sat in her lap, straddling her. Naturally her hands gripped my arse as I let out a breathy moan.

'I'm only hungry for one thing, V. Give it to me, please,' I pleaded.

'Oh, Sunshine, you never need to beg with me. Whatever, whenever. It's yours. I'm yours.' Those words had me clenching my thighs around her, dragging her lips to mine, tangling my fingers in that soft hair of hers. It felt like water running through my fingers; I wanted her but felt like I couldn't fully grasp her.

Suddenly, we were up and moving across my apartment until I felt the plush blankets of my bed as I was thrown onto my back. I laughed at the sudden, playful jolt.

V took a step back, taking me in and licking her lips as she took off her red satin blazer and dropped it on the floor. This woman must be rich if she could treat satin like that. Slowly she undid her matching slacks, stepping out of them so sensually she gave my dancing a run for its money. The only thing left was a white camisole and as she raised it I realised she wore nothing underneath. No underwear: she was bare and suddenly I couldn't breathe. V's body was unlike any woman's I had ever seen, and I had seen many in my line of work.

Where my hips were narrow, hers were wider but they tapered into thin legs that rivalled my own. Her stomach was real, not the taut concave nonsense that us dancers slaved away at the gym to create. No, there was something for me to grip and hold as petite as she was. And those breasts were perfection; the way they lightly moved as her body did had me salivating, wanting a touch and a taste.

Though the most breathtaking part about her was the tattoos. Under her clothes, you would never know that nearly every part of her skin that she could hide was covered in a patchwork of black ink. I had never liked tattoos much, but here and now, they were the most attractive things I had ever seen on any person.

Climbing on top of me, she held herself there absorbing this minute in time, then she dived down, tasting my lips. I could never get used to the feeling of her tongue exploring my mouth—it was warm and sensual in all of the best ways.

Her hands found their way to my hips, gripping them on the edge of pain that was still pleasure, but so close to something more that it stirred something within me. I wanted to be claimed by this woman. I had been with possessive men before, but this was different. I felt wanted by V, not like my body was just a means to an end to satisfy some dark, twisted need for control.

With her, I felt in control, so to test that, I paused and pulled back, stilling her. Instead of continuing, she halted, looking at me and assessing what was wrong and what I needed.

'Tell me why. Tell me why you want me,' I breathed.

'Because I want to unravel you. I need to understand the contradiction between that brilliant smile and those pained eyes. Because even though I barely know you, an instinct pulls at me to protect you, to make you happy because when you are, my God, do I feel it too. Because every look, touch and word from you turns my mind and body into molten lava. No one, absolutely no one, has made me feel a tenth of what you do. Because your soul calls to mine, and I know I can give you what you need, but more than that, what you deserve.'

That was enough and without much thought I plunged my hand down between her legs. Instead of pushing me back and reclaiming control, she let me indulge in what I wanted and the feel of her slick wetness had me groaning in satisfaction. Her words were one thing, but her body couldn't lie; she truly did want me, maybe more than I wanted her, and that gave me the sense of safety I needed right now. I could walk away, and I knew in my soul she would let me, unlike with Jason.

Her back arched as my fingers slid in and out of her. She leaned forward, arms shaking, as I brought her closer to a pleasure so rich it shattered her. I sunk my teeth into her neck and held them there, pressing harder and harder as she came closer and closer.

She panted wildly, breathing erratic as she lost her composure on top of me. She was mine. No one had ever been mine before; this was the first time I felt the power of owning someone, and I loved the thrill of it.

A more sinister part of me wanted to stop right now and

leave her on the edge, but another part of me wanted to see what she looked like as she came apart for me the way I had for her in the Velvet Room. The latter side of me won out as I slammed my fingers back into her and curled them, stroking the bundle of nerves inside her, over and over. Her moan turned into a feral scream as her muscles tightened and the sound died out as the spike of pleasure continued to rock through her. Then her body relaxed and sunk down onto mine.

'Well, that's a first,' she huffed, catching her breath as she rolled onto her back beside me, staring up at the ceiling.

'What is?'

'No one has ever been able to give me an orgasm before. Not to mention, you're the first woman I've ever been with. You're claiming a few of my firsts here, Sunshine,' she said through a smile. Propping myself up on my elbow, I looked down at her, trying to determine if what she was telling me was the truth, but there was no hint of a lie on her face.

'I've never been with a woman either,' I said, unable to hide the grin from my face as I noticed the shock on hers.

'Well, you had me fooled. Those fingers seemed… experienced.' She smirked.

'Nope, just a natural.' I batted my lashes as we fell into a fit of laughter.

'Let's see how I measure up, then shall we?' V breathed into my ear, pushing me down onto the bed as she moved herself between my legs. Warmth enveloped my slit as her tongue dragged across it slowly before flicking across my clit, forcing my back to arch off the bed, chasing that caress before she dove back down, teasing me with slow strokes of her tongue. A deep groan left her lips as she dipped her tongue inside me.

'You taste like heaven, my little ray of Sunshine. I've never tasted anything better in my life. I could bury myself right here until the end of time.' My fingers slid into her hair and pulled her lips over my clit, chasing more of that intensity. She tried to swallow every drip of my wetness as though she was dehydrated and I was the first bit of water she had seen in days. She seemed to get just as much satisfaction out of pleasing me as I did.

I rode her face as my hips bucked into her, chasing that high. I felt nails pressing into my thighs as she buried herself deeper. Insatiable with thirst, our eyes locked, and the fire in her gaze nearly sent me over the edge. Just as I screamed the beginnings of an orgasm that was crawling up my spine, she stilled, pulling back. As a whine escaped my lips, she plunged her fingers into me as she straddled my hips; her own hips moved in time with her hand as she ground against the air, feeling every moment of my pleasure as if it was her own. Her left hand wrapped around my throat, pushing me into the bed and squeezing as her fingers slid in and out of me so fast I lost all sense of reality. My hips stilled, no longer having to chase anything, because she was delivering exactly what I needed on a golden platter.

My insides clenched as I neared that edge once more.

'Harder,' I gasped through her hand, restraining my neck. In response, she increased her rhythm, but I shook my head. I wanted her to squeeze harder, to choke me so that every memory of passing out from my past could be erased and replaced by this moment with her, where it was my choice. She responded in kind, keeping me on the edge of consciousness.

'V, I'm so close.' I pleaded—for what, I wasn't sure, but

instinctively I knew that she would edge me once more. Ignoring me, she stilled again, pulling her fingers from me and releasing my neck. As she looked at the panting, writhing mess I had become on the bed, locking eyes with me, she opened her mouth and sucked my wetness from her fingers. Then, eyes closing, she moaned over the way I tasted.

'What do you want, Sunshine? Tell me exactly.'

'I want to come. Please let me come,' I begged.

'Such a good fucking girl.' She smirked as she leaned forward, gripping my hair, pulling my head to the side. As her teeth grazed over my ear, her fingers circled ever so slowly around my clit. Electricity shot through me as I all but spasmed beneath her touch. She kept her touch light and slow, mimicking the feather-light kisses she trailed down my neck.

Increasing the pace of her fingers, she dragged the skin of my neck into her mouth and sucked. I lost control of my body and, instead of chasing that feeling, I found myself almost curling away from the sheer intensity of her thrumming over my clit in perfect increasing rhythm. I lost the ability to think, speak or even moan. My whole body was taut, coiling in anticipation, building with each trace of my clit as the pressure in my neck built and the cord snapped, shattering me. As an ungodly scream ripped itself from my core, I braced myself against her body.

I hadn't realised my vision had faded until suddenly I could see again. Tears rolled from my eyes—unbidden—from such a pure pleasure I had never felt before as my skin vibrated over me. My body couldn't comprehend it, so I cried. V kissed every tear that spilled from my eyes and licked her lips, savouring the taste of what she had done to my body and mind. Rebuilding me in this moment as wholly hers.

We spent the next half hour in silence; I felt nothing but safety and warmth envelop me as she held me close. She didn't probe or push to know what I had been musing over or what had triggered the tears; she knew they weren't from anything bad. She had read me from the moment she met me. She could see that it was my body not understanding how to process pure happiness that wasn't tainted by anything else. Tainted by that pain I carried, that she saw without having to dig.

We fell asleep in each other's arms, and when the sun rose, I sleepily blinked my eyes open. V was lying in bed watching me. Sunlight streaked through the large windows, making me squint.

'This, right here, is what I want every day until my last day. My little ray of Sunshine, lying naked in the sunshine. You're breathtaking.' Our lips collided and my sleepy limbs were a slow fumbling mess, pulling her closer. I had never been treated like this by anyone and I loved it. Being worshiped like this healed parts of my soul long forgotten.

'Sorry morning breath. Shit, I have work, V. I need to get ready. I wish I could call in sick,' I groaned. She kissed me once more, deeper this time, her tongue reaching every inch of mine. Clearly, she didn't mind.

'So call in sick.'

'Absolutely not. My boss from the club got me that job and he is absolutely fucking terrifying. He's a good man, don't get me wrong, but he is not someone I ever want to cross, let alone disrespect by taking for granted the opportunity he gave me. He vouched for me even when he didn't know me. A man like that values his word and reputation above all else. I don't feel like being skinned alive when I've just found so much to live for.' I beamed at her as the last thought escaped my lips unbidden.

V laughed but nodded, pulling me from the bed as she found her clothes. She'd likely heard the rumours about the man and family who ran this city.

# 7
# VALENTINA

The rest of the day after dropping Namazzi off was spent holed up in my studio, finishing the painting of her. The red she had chosen was the perfect colour for her lingerie. When I stepped away, I felt the captivating stare of my girl, the warmth of her smile and the suppleness of her skin, as if she were here with me now. It was my best piece. I had been painting for as long as I could remember, but this was the first time the painting truly came alive. This would be my show. It would centre around Sunshine, my muse.

V: Are you working tonight?

Sunshine: No, but I don't think we should see each other again.

Not this again. How could she be retreating once more after such a perfect night together? I knew for a fact that she wanted me nearly as much as I wanted her. The voices in her head and the self-doubt could not have changed her mind this quickly. No, something must have happened. This was fear speaking but fear of what I wasn't sure.

I had been planning to throw on the wheel; I wanted to create a vase for my girl for her eclectic apartment. While rifling through her cupboards in search of plates, I realised she didn't have one, and if I wanted to give her flowers, she would need one. There was no point in creating one if she shut me out, so I couldn't let that happen.

When I got to the store, I found a stranger behind the register who said Sunshine had left not long after her shift had begun. Speeding to her apartment, a sinking feeling settled in my stomach.

I slammed on her door, calling her name, but there was no response. Fear crept up my spine and tickled my mind. Calling her phone, there was no answer, but I could hear the faint vibrations on the other side of the door.

I looked for spare keys under the mat but there was nothing. I had two options: smash down the door to check if she was okay, or call the landlord, but that would take too long. My mind went through every worst-case scenario imaginable.

Taking a deep breath and remembering that I was the youngest member of a criminal empire, I pulled the miniature lock-picking kit Z had gifted me from my keys and began working on picking her lock. Was I, quite possibly, insane at that moment for trying to break into the home of the girl who said she didn't want to see me anymore? Yes, especially considering I barely knew her. But this wasn't selfish now; no, I was worried about her. Something didn't feel right and if there was one thing I learned from my brothers, was to trust my instincts. If she truly wanted me gone, she wouldn't have left an opening by telling me she was off work tonight. She wouldn't have been off sick, and she would be opening this door right now to tell me to fuck off if that's what she wanted. She wouldn't cower from me; she was emboldened by me, taking exactly what she wanted from me. Nervous at times, yes, but never scared to face me.

The door clicked as the final internal pieces unlocked. Walking inside the apartment was dark, with massive curtains drawn, covering the vast windows and casting shadows in the early afternoon. I called for her, but there was no response. Flicking on the lights, I found the little studio empty. Her phone was on the kitchen counter, accompanied by a slightly unnerving number of missed calls. Two were from me, but the other twenty were from an unknown number. Instinctively, I knew what had caused this—something or rather, someone from her past that she had been running from had finally caught up with her.

The sound of the shower drew me in; the door was wide open, and there my Sunshine sat on the floor of her shower —naked, bruised, and lifeless except for the rise and fall of her chest. She stared blankly at the tiles, neither seeing me nor noticing my presence.

Her deep skin was a muddled mess of bruises that covered nearly every limb and the side of her body. Her lip was split but there didn't appear to be anything visibly broken. Blood was caked beneath her nails and mascara streaked her face. My poor girl.

Stepping under the spray fully clothed I pulled her into my lap holding her, letting her feel my promise, that I would never let her go. I was here; I was hers, and nothing would ever hurt her again. She didn't react, remaining stuck in the dark recesses of her mind. So much time passed that the water turned cold. Gently I carried her to the bed, placing her down with a towel wrapped around her as I found her something warm to wear. Then I clothed her and tucked her under the covers, before sending a quick text to my brother.

Slowly I peeled my own soaking wet clothes off and as they hit the floor with a loud squelch her head snapped up, drawing her focus. Her cloudy eyes became clearer. She watched me undress, mouth agape, brows furrowed in confusion. As if noticing my presence for the first time today and not quite understanding whether I was real or just a figment of her imagination, she took me in. I threw on an oversized shirt of hers on then bundled up with her under the covers, holding her close. She gripped me tightly as she tried to hold back the sobs that finally escaped her body. It wasn't the physical pain of the marks left on her body. No, this was a heart-wrenching pain that came with losing a part of your soul; her heart was breaking for herself right now and I vowed I would piece it back together.

'Sunshine, please tell me what happened. I need to know,' I asked when her sobbing calmed as I stroked along her back in soothing circles. She took a few deep breaths, finally looking back at me. She was in turmoil; I could see every emotion flickering through those beautiful, deep brown eyes. Gone was her signature grin; her face was slack with exhaustion now.

'Why are you here, V?' she asked, starting to pull away as she remembered the message she had sent. But even as her mind told her body to create distance between us, I felt her hands tighten over my shirt, not wanting to let go.

'I'm here because I was worried about you. I knew that

message was bullshit, darling. I went to your work to check what had happened and they told me you went home sick. I knew something was wrong; I'm just sorry I was right. Now you need to get over this notion that you're going to push me away and deal with this by yourself. I know I sound insane right now Sunshine, but I think I love you. I think I fell in love with you the moment our eyes locked at that club, and you have overtaken every fibre of my being since. So, I'm not going anywhere. Not when I know you want me too.' The tears streaked down her face again as she buried herself in my shoulder. Stroking her wet braids, I hummed, trying to sooth her.

'I mean it, Sunshine. I love you. Now let me help you.' She wasn't ready. Not just yet. Gently removing her hands from me I stepped back into her bathroom and grabbed a few supplies before laying them out on her bedside table. I needed to show her how much I cared, not simply declare it hoping she would believe it. Picking up the microfibre towel I squeezed the excess moisture starting from the roots to the ends of her braids. Once I removed as much as I could I used the hairdryer to dry the rest. It didn't take long for her to settle into the moment. Once there wasn't a lick of moisture left, I used the oil blend I found. A mixture of tea tree oil and jojoba and massaged it into her scalp, gently working the oil in. She fully relaxed into me then as the last of her tears dried.

Slowly she composed herself but kept her head down; whatever she had to say was layered in shame. She couldn't look at me, but whatever it was, it wasn't her shame to bear. Cupping her chin, I tilted her head up, locking her eyes on mine.

Swallowing, she gathered her courage. 'It was Jason, my ex. He saw us in the morning. I thought he had skipped town after my boss threatened him the last time he came by the club, but apparently, he's been watching me. I didn't even know he knew where my new apartment was; I thought I was safe. He was angry, though, after... he saw us kiss. He came in while I was still setting up the store. He said I was his, that I would always be his, and that it was bad enough I whored around for a job; now I was just a common street slut. H-He said he would kill you; he'd make me watch and then I would know my place. That he owned me and that I could never find happiness with anyone else. He would always be there. Th-then he beat me until I apologised. I refused but it just made him angrier and the hits harder, but I couldn't apologise. It felt like denying us and I didn't want to. He sent that message from my phone. It wasn't me, but now maybe it should have been.'

I had to hold back my laugh at his threat to kill me; I'd love to see him try. I may not be as deep into the underworld as my brothers were, because I had other goals, but I had trained alongside them. They knew I would never be wholly safe and they wanted me to know what to do if the worst ever happened.

I kissed her gently, mindful of her split lip. 'You're not a whore. You're not his. You belong to no one. He will not hurt me and I promise you, Sunshine, he will never hurt you again.' I kissed her forehead, then each cheek, followed by her chin and then the tip of her nose, so delicately, lovingly. I hoped she could hear the conviction in my voice and feel it with every touch. I had no doubts that I had spoken nothing but the truth. I would protect her.

'Collect your things, you're coming home with me. It's not safe for you here.' She began to shake her head, trying to find a good argument, but I stopped her.

'I know you have been fighting this battle alone for a

long time, but right now, you need to trust me. Trust that I have got you. Please let me keep you safe. I can't leave you here.'

She looked into my eyes and saw that there would be no winning this one, so I packed a bag as she pointed to the things she needed most. This morning, when I left her place, I had been planning to invite her to dinner to meet my brothers. Now, it turned out that it would happen much sooner than expected. Although I had wished it would be under better circumstances for her sake. I didn't know how she would react to meeting them. I felt I should give her some warning, but she seemed exhausted. It could wait.

# 8
# VALENTINA

The house was empty. I knew my brothers would be out all night working, but Z had already sent me a million texts trying to push for more details as to why Namazzi wouldn't be able to attend work for the foreseeable future, assuring me that he would sort it out.

As we entered, Sunshine marveled at the modern interior. Each of us had our own level and only shared the common spaces, but even those were large enough to provide us with ample space when needed. I could feel her skin crawl with discomfort at how different her apartment had been in comparison. It was the same look she had when she'd seen my car. She knew I was well off, but it wasn't until she took in the large marble countertops, high ceilings and luxurious furniture that she understood just how wealthy I was.

She quickly crashed after a warm bath and a glass of wine. She looked breathtaking on my four-poster bed. My room was nothing but black-stained wood, emerald-green velvet, and gothic décor, and amidst it all, she was a beacon of light, my little ray of sunshine. My brothers had laughed when I decorated it assuming I would opt for colour given my penchant for artistry. After looking at vivid colours all day, I liked the solitude and calm deeper and darker colours brought. It allowed my brain to switch off.

At some point, I dozed off, and when I awoke, my girl was trembling in her sleep as the early morning sun streamed through the gaps in the curtains. She was having a fitful nightmare. Slowly I coaxed her out of it, stroking her hair to rouse her until her bleary eyes locked on mine. She was confused for a moment but then, as she took me in, her signature smile returned before she winced in pain, the cut on her lip cracking open once again. I licked up the drop of blood as it pooled on her lips.

'Sunshine,' I breathed against her ear. Her body shuddered in response. She pulled herself up, wanting to crawl into my lap, to be held. I let her.

'I didn't get a chance to tell you last night but I live with my brothers. Now don't panic—they know you're here, but I didn't say anything. That's your story to tell. You won't see them, though, unless you want to join us for meals. We each have our own level in this building. But... I want to know how you would like me to introduce you. I know what you are to me but I don't know what I am to you.' Her cheeks flushed as her eyes darted away.

Barely above a whisper she asked, 'What am I to you?'

Without hesitation, the word fell from my lips. 'Everything.' Nodding, she took in the word, letting it settle into her bones.

She pulled my face to hers, placing a chaste kiss on my lips, branding me with her piercing eyes. They were the most alive I had seen them since I found her on the floor of her shower, looking at me with a certainty that I had never seen in her before. It was as if she had finally made an irrevocable decision.

'Everything,' she breathed.

After that we held each other in bed, watching the rest of the sunrise. We spoke about our dreams while whispering sweet nothings to one another. Not ready to talk about anything real yet. We wanted to ride out this happy moment where we had claimed one another. After texting into work to say she wouldn't be there, not knowing I had already taken that liberty, she agreed to meet my brothers for a lunch. I messaged the boys to come home and asked Xavier to order in her favourite cuisine—Japanese.

It wasn't long before lunch. Zane had said he would be a couple of minutes late, so we headed down to set the table and pick out a bottle of wine from the cellar. She was partial to a deep, robust red like myself, settling on a Malbec. I had dismissed Evelyn wanting to give my girl as much privacy as I could while she both mentally and physically recovered from yesterday.

As we poured our wine, I prepared to rip the Band Aid off and tell my girl exactly who my family was. She seemed calmer now, but I waited too long. Xavier walked into the kitchen.

'Food's set up in the dining room if you two ladies are ready,' he said. Walking towards her with his arm outstretched, he shook her hand.

'I'm Xavier, you are?'

'Namazzi.'

His eyes took in the split of her lips and the cuts on her hands; every other bruise was covered by my favourite track pants and jumper I had given her. Xavier's eyes flickered to mine in question, concern etched on his features, but he didn't probe, instead sweeping her into the dining room as I trailed behind them.

'Wow, what's all this? Are we celebrating something?' she asked, taking a seat beside me as Xavier took the one across from her. He knew Zane was intimidating, to say the least, so he thought it would be best if she wasn't directly facing him. Too bad he didn't know they already knew each other.

'We're celebrating you, Sunshine. It's rare that I bring anyone home, so I wanted to do something nice,' I explained. Her cheeks flushed as she flashed me her winning smile.

'You shouldn't have, V. It's too much.'

Ignoring her, I filled her plate with all of her favourites that we had spoken about during our first date at Guido's: salmon sashimi, scallops, thinly sliced teriyaki beef and a katsu chicken curry with pickled daikon.

'So how do you two know each other? Better yet, who are you to each other?' my brother asked, looking between the two of us. My girl tensed, fearing the judgement that typically came with her line of work, which she didn't realise she would never find here. Leaning into her side, I grabbed her hand under the table and nudged her shoulder.

'This is my everything,' I said to my brother, but my eyes never left hers.

'I suppose I should cancel your engagement then.' Xavier chuckled as my girl choked on her wine.

'Xav!' I scolded. 'He's lying, Sunshine. I'm not engaged. It's a bit more complicated than that.' Slowly, she swallowed, composing herself as I shot daggers at Xav. I knew what he was doing; he was testing me. Teasing me. Not her.

Before I could explain any further, Zane blew through the door.

*Shit.* I hadn't found the time to tell Sunshine, and now she was confronted and cornered.

She stood, shooting out of her chair and backing away. Zane looked pissed, as though he were on a war path, but that was just his demeanour and partially my fault for not replying to his messages. He hadn't even really taken in who our guest was yet. Her sudden movement drew his attention just before he went to sit down.

I stood, blocking her from his view. I wanted her to feel safe.

Xav was the first to break the tense silence. 'What am I missing here?'

Sunshine spoke first, but it was directed at Zane. 'Wh-what are you doing here? Is this because I called in sick?' She looked petrified.

Turning, I grabbed her by the shoulders. 'This is on me, Sunshine. I was going to tell you. Zane... he's my brother.'

'WHAT?' she shrieked.

Zane exploded into a fit of laughter. 'I see you made your decision, sister.' He smirked and I rolled my eyes at him.

Sunshine pushed out of my arms, taking a step back then looking between us. 'Y-you're a De Luca?!'

'Yes and no. We're blood. I share their last name but I'm not a "De Luca",' I said, making quotation marks with my hands to emphasise the difference. 'I don't really have a role in the family businesses. I might... help from time to time, and these two tried to marry me off to other families to gain some more territory because I wasn't really seeing anyone until now. But, that's not my life, Sunshine. It's theirs. However, there are benefits, like being able to castrate the man that did this to you. So... will you forgive me? I didn't mean to hide it from you, not really,' I pleaded, stepping closer into her.

'This is... a lot to take in,' she breathed.

Zane spoke then after he seemed to take in what my last comment had meant. 'Jason's back?' he asked.

Xav went to interject, asking who that was.

'Her ex,' Zane and I said in unison.

'She's going to be staying here from now on. Xav, find him. Zane, end him. Also, Sunshine here will be taking a leave of absence from both roles until this is sorted. But Z, you make sure her jobs are still there when she's ready, if she wants them.'

'Wait, wait, wait. You can't just go deciding these things on your own, V. It's my life! And what do you mean, "end him"?'

'You know what I mean; you know our name and what we do. We will make sure this never happens again. I just want to keep you safe, baby girl.' I soothed her by pulling her into my arms.

Her body was still tense, and she seemed uncertain, but she had claimed me just as much as I had claimed her, and I wasn't going anywhere. I knew we were in front of my brothers, but I refused to hide any part of my love for her; she carried enough shame. I needed to be proud of her.

'Let yourself think long enough, and there will be a million reasons not to, but I promise I can give you a million more reasons why we should. Do not let the voices win this one. You deserve safety, you deserve love, you deserve to be happy,' I whispered into the crook of her neck. 'You've never allowed yourself to freefall into something like this, but here and now you can. Give in; no more rationalising or overthinking. Just *feel*. Let that guide you; guide us. Sunshine, I'm yours. I don't know how many more times I can convince you of this. Let go. Live in the fantasy if you need to until it becomes reality. What do you say?'

Her answer was a searing kiss that had me pulling her into my body until she winced, and then I remembered myself and the two men we stood in front of. Zane looked *almost* proud. He was a monster in the truest sense of the word, but he had a soft centre buried deep, especially for his little sister.

Xav took us in one more time, acceptance finally settling in. 'Welcome to the family, Namazzi. Would you like your own room? Perhaps your own level? We can look at remodelling the guest level to suite your tastes, otherwise you can stay with V in her space. As for Jason, it seems Zane already has the information that I'll need to start my investigation, seeing as he's tried to deal with this situation himself before, I'm assuming?'

'Just like that? You're what, exactly? Accepting me? Fighting for me? You don't care that I'm not good enough for your sister? I have no money—I'm a stripper for Christ's sake!' She was stunned.

Z chose to respond then. 'Just like that. You get involved with one of us, you get all of us. As for who isn't good enough for whom, it's V who's going to have to prove she's worth you. I already warned her once. She breaks your heart; I break her legs. No one, absolutely no one, fucks with my girls, Namazzi—not even my family. And you don't need money; we have more than enough. That's how it works in this family: everyone owns everything. As for the stripper comment, really? You won't find judgement from me for surviving by any means necessary. V sure as fuck doesn't care. If anything, it probably works in her favour. And as for our stoic older brother, if you knew him on a personal level, you would be the one judging him and his sex life. No one here in this room, no matter the material possessions we have, is in a position to judge you. We wouldn't even think to—'

Xav interrupted then. 'It's true. We couldn't care less. Besides, if I'm being honest, I was worried V wouldn't find someone decent in this lifetime because of us. Because of who we are, there are only a few who would attempt to claim her, but she always deserved better. In my line of work, Namazzi, you get good at reading people and I see right through you. You're going to be good for her. Besides, I should be thanking you because you see her for who she is —not her name, money or power. I see the way you look at each other. It's real. And you're not sitting here judging us for what we do and how we use our bodies; is far more sinister. So, we're good.'

# 9
# SUNSHINE

I couldn't believe this family, and I was pretty sure they were all slightly unstable. But then, so was I, because V was right. I wanted to live in this fantasy world with her and I was done denying myself. I believed her when she said she was mine, and for the first time ever, I wanted to be owned and wholly someone else's. She was the first person who didn't take from me, and that made me want to give her everything.

I decided in that moment that I would never doubt these feelings or us again. She was my everything, and I would let this family burn the world to ashes to protect what I had found in her. Hope. Love. Safety. Turning to her, I cupped her cheeks and felt the gentle thud of her forehead as it rested on mine.

Whispering so only she could hear, I said the words that would seal this new string of fate. 'I love you.'

Before I could do anything else, her lips crashed into mine, and the floor disappeared from under me as V swept me up into her arms. She strode us towards the table, placing me on its edge and pulling my legs in one quick movement as she stepped between them, pressing against me.

'Out!' she shouted, as embarrassment rushed over me. I had forgotten that we weren't alone. I heard them both chuckle before the door clicked shut behind them.

V kissed down my neck. 'Say it again,' she pleaded, pulling my chin to meet her gaze. Her eyes were ragged with emotion.

'I'm yours, V. Wholly and completely yours, from this moment until the end. I love you.'

A groan escaped her lips as she ground her hips into mine before plunging her fingers into my pants. 'Fuck, Sunshine, if I had known you weren't wearing anything under these, I wouldn't have even let you come down here. We would have been stuck upstairs this whole time doing exactly this. You drive me fucking crazy.'

Without hesitation, she slid a finger inside me; I was wet and I didn't need any coaxing. Her raw, unfiltered need was enough for me.

She added another finger as my back arched. I still didn't quite understand how those long nails of hers never hurt me when she was inside me, but she glided through me knowing exactly where to touch.

'Say it,' she gritted as she held her fingers just outside my slit, barely grazing it, teasing me.

'I love you.'

The second the words left my lips she slammed into me before drawing them out and pausing. 'Again,' she commanded.

'I love you,' I breathed. I felt her fingers brush against my walls—filling me, going deep, reaching for my fucking soul. Not letting me relish in the sensation for long before she pulled completely out of me once more. I whimpered, wanting more from her.

'Again.'

*Fuck, she was going to edge me.*

'I love you.' I barely got the words out, too distracted by the empty feeling; my core clenched, trying to find something but finding nothing. I found relief as her fingers slid back in and curled inside me but this time she didn't pull out. They sat inside me, millimeters from that sweet spot that would have my world shattering. I lifted my hips trying to get her deeper; I needed her to touch that one spot.

'Tell me why and don't stop unless you want me to stop,' she ground out. I could tell this was torturing her just as much as it was me and that sent a powerful thrill through me. Her fingers began to thrum but my lips weren't moving. She stilled again, waiting until her words sunk in.

'Your eyes—the way you look at me, hungry. Your touch—it sends lightning through my veins. Your body—stunning; every curve, every tattoo is breathtaking to look at. The way you care about me, consider what I want first. The way you always give me the option, the control. The way you view me, like I'm worthy, like I have value, like I'm special. The way I know you would burn the world to the ground for me. The way you make me want to do the same for you. The way our bodies fit so perfectly. Fuck, fuck, fuck, oh my god, V! I can't...'

Waves of pleasure crashed through me as her finger traced that one special spot within me and had my body detonating. Lightly, she stroked the spot, wringing out every last pulse of pleasure from me.

'The way I connect with you, like I've always known you,

like we were born with the sole purpose of meeting one day, and that I was incomplete, living a half-life until I met you. I love you because every second with you feels right, feels safe. Like we were meant to be. I love you'—I kissed her—'because of your passion, your confidence, your pure determination. Because you consume my mind and every waking thought and just thinking about you has become my happy place in a world that's stripped too much away from me. Because you make me feel both safe and alive at the same time. I just fucking love you, V. Because you're everything.' There was that word again. There was no other way to describe her, or us, and what this had become in such a short amount of time.

'Then make me feel it.' Her words were my undoing. I got up, pushing her down onto the table. I would show her exactly how I revered her. How much I valued her. I kissed her lips gently at first, the softness beckoning me to kiss a little harder, to drag that supple flesh between my teeth and bite. The feel of her tongue was warm and inviting, coaxing me deeper, wanting to consume her. The kiss turned desperate before I pulled back, dragging her bottom lip between my teeth.

Letting her catch her breath, I moved down to her neck. And as I sucked her flesh into my mouth, drawing her blood to the surface, she moaned arching into me. Kissing down her chest, I lavished attention on her breasts. Flicking her nipple with my tongue until it pebbled, I grazed my teeth over it, drawing a breathy moan from her. Moving to the next breast, I did the same thing. Her nails dug into my shoulders as she desperately tried to hold onto reality while sinking further into her pleasure. I drew more of her into my mouth and sucked watching her back arch once more. Pretty thing liked that, I wondered if she would like the feeling elsewhere.

My lips trailed down her body ever so teasingly; I wanted her needy beneath me. I wanted to be wholly in control, and she was so close to losing herself to me and what I could give her. V let out a frustrated cry as I grazed my lips back and forth over the inside of her thigh, drawing closer, before pulling back. My hands stroked the outside of her thighs and her skin erupted into little bumps of delight.

Edging closer I exhaled over the slit between her legs and that sweet little clit of hers that would have her losing her mind in seconds if touched right. She whimpered—actually fucking whimpered—under me and it drove me feral as she slid her fingers into my hair, pulling me flush with her body, not allowing me to escape her clutches and the pleasure I promised.

I chuckled; this is exactly how I wanted her—what I had been building to. She wanted me to show her, and I would. Barely touching her, my tongue almost hovered over her as I licked up her slit. I knew it wouldn't be enough. Her fingers pulled harder and that touch of pain went straight to my molten core, making me almost as wet and needy as her.

This time, I pressed my flattened tongue against her and laved at her, wanting every last drop of that almost metallic taste. Nothing compared to it; I wanted to drink it, be covered in it and inhale it. I strummed my tongue over her clit and watched as her body tightened and squirmed. The pressure I had built in her body was making her overly sensitive. Wanting to push her further, I pushed a finger inside her.

'Fuck!' she gasped, bucking off the table and chasing my finger as I drew out. This time, I pushed into her with two. My hands were much smaller than V's, so I knew I could fit more inside her, and I wanted to see just how many that was. I wanted to make her my own personal puppet, completely controlling her. I *needed* it. To feel that power after I had been stripped of mine again and again.

As I thrust my fingers into her, she raised her hips to meet me. I pressed her back down, my hand splayed just below her stomach, stilling her. My thumb brushed over her clit a couple times in warning. If she wanted this, I would set the pace. I was about to give her exactly what she wanted and then some.

I plunged a third finger inside of her as she cried out, completely euphoric. I stayed inside her and curled my fingers up over that sweet spot inside of her. Her whole body shuddered as I used my other hand to press down a touch more, so that I could almost feel my fingers curl inside of her from the outside. Her pleasure ratcheted up, and she began to pant, moaning as she lost herself under my touch.

She was close; I felt it in the way her body coiled, ready to explode. I pulled out at the very last second before I knew she would tip over that edge and her body would take her with it whether I wanted it to or not. She almost screamed in frustration, but no sound came out. Instead, a single tear trailed down her face. I licked it and savoured the taste of salt on my tongue. I had never had this power over someone, and it thrilled me. She had given me this.

A thought struck me then: I enjoyed her crying under me, controlling her, punishing her. Was I just as bad as Jason? No. I didn't want to hurt her; I don't think I ever could. This was all about pleasure—her pleasure—and knowing that I was creating so much turmoil in her body that she would detonate like a euphoric explosion, overwhelming all of her senses. I would sear myself into her soul and body, ruining her for anyone else. She would never be able to have anyone touch her again without remembering me, and how good I made her feel.

I slammed my three fingers back into her and drew them back out just as quickly, repeating the rhythm over and over again. I glided through her as she soaked me in her wetness. My other hand roamed over her body, pulling on a nipple before finding her neck and gripping it. She loved a touch of pain with her pleasure—just like I did—and I would give it to her. I squeezed just hard enough that she had to hold her breath. Her eyes burned into mine as I continued pushing into her at an ungodly rhythm. I watched as that fire in her eyes fluttered. The black dots in her vision undoubtedly creeping in further as the room faded and all that was left was me slamming into her repeatedly as I wrung the pleasure from her body.

Easing my grip off of her neck, I slammed into her deeper than I had before, touching that sweet spot that had her body exploding as a guttural scream left her. She gushed on her dining room floor and I dove between her legs, licking at the liquid as it dripped down her thighs. She tasted fucking incredible.

I let her catch her breath, watching the rapid rise and fall of her chest. Pulling her up, I had to almost hold her so she wouldn't slip from the table.

'Did you feel it?' I asked, kissing that soft spot on her neck under her ear.

'Yes,' she cried as she smiled at me, tears streaming down her face. Panic roared through me.

'What's wrong, V? Why are you crying? What did I do?' I asked, clasping her face between my hands, pleading with her.

'Nothing—it was absolutely perfect. I've just never experienced anything like that; I think my body is overwhelmed. These are happy tears, Sunshine,' she said, kissing me reassuringly. I let out a sigh of relief, letting my forehead meet hers as I breathed her in.

'Let's eat and get cleaned up. I want to take you somewhere,' V said, using my body to steady herself. Only now did the sinking feeling of the fact that I had just fucked her on the dining room table she shared with her brothers—the same brothers who were currently in this very house.

'Please tell me these walls are soundproof,' I groaned. She laughed but nodded as relief washed over me. *Thank God.*

'We learnt that lesson the hard way after we overheard Xav in a rather compromising position. We ended up renovating the whole house with soundproofing to be careful.'

# 10
# VALENTINA

Since the moment my little ray of Sunshine told me her dream was to be a gallery director, I wanted to bring her to my gallery and studio. I was ready to lay it all on the line, more so than I had already done—if that was even possible. I wanted her to know just how far this ran for me—that this was forever. She knew the depth of my feelings, but we hadn't discussed what truly comes next. Where we went from here.

When we got out of my car, she looked at me quizzically. 'What's this? I thought this place was undergoing renovations. I've walked past it so many times on my lunch breaks. There shouldn't be any shows on.'

'This is my studio space... and my gallery.' She stared at me, wide-eyed, as I unlocked the door and held it open for her. I let her go first, wanting to see her reaction to the expansive space. It was a clean slate that would be filled with my works soon enough.

'This is incredible. I've never seen anything like it. You could do so much with this space.'

'*We* could do so much.'

She looked at me dubiously, as if she hadn't quite heard me properly. I snuck in behind her, wrapped my arms around her waist, and nuzzled my chin into that soft spot where her neck met her shoulders.

'I want this to be ours, Sunshine. You can do what you want when we get rid of Jason.' She flinched at the casual threat but shook it off just as quickly.

'I never started my search for a gallery director. I couldn't even bring myself to create anything and then you fell into my life—my muse. Suddenly, I could paint again. I was inspired and everything, it all circled back to you. I don't want to do this without you. I know it may be too much, but I'm all in. Everything to me also means forever. I want to intertwine our lives; I want you to be a part of my dream and I want to be a part of yours. If you want to go back to the art shop or the club, I won't stop you, but I want you to know that I would love to have you here with me.'

She turned around, stepping back and looking at me dumbfounded.

'I have no experience. How can I run a gallery this big when I've never done this a day in my life? I would ruin this for you. I would wreck your dream, V.'

Shaking my head, I pulled her to the back, down the hallway and up the stairs. Once she saw my work, she would understand.

Her breath hitched taking in the largest studio she had probably set eyes on and my god the reality of her being here was sweeter than my fantasies. I loved this place because of the large windows and the natural light that shone through from every direction. Watching my ray of sunshine walk by, she looked ethereal, glowing golden as the sun kissed her rich skin. It was enough to make my knees weak, as if I could collapse at her feet.

She let out a gasp upon seeing it. In the center of the room was my latest painting. It was quite literally the size of my car, and the image I depicted was unmistakable. It was her. It was a masterpiece of swirling brushstrokes that conveyed life and movement. It was her walking ahead of me down a hallway, hand outstretched, reaching for me as she looked over her shoulder with that goddamn perfect smile of hers and captivating eyes. That red lingerie criss-crossing over the planes of her back as her coiled hair bounced with every step.

'It's me,' she whispered, stepping closer and taking in every detail. The texture of the oil paints, along with the shift in colours as the light hit it from a different angles. The hallway was dark behind her, but she stood out like the sun.

'I started painting this after I met you. That day, I met you in the shop to buy paint. It was for this—for the red lace you were wearing. I didn't have a collection to fill this place until I met you, but now I know exactly what I want to create. You don't need experience to curate our love Sunshine. There is no one better suited to run this gallery and showcase this work than you. It wouldn't exist without you. It has to be you.'

She was stunned, but it didn't take long for her to compose herself, letting out a slow exhale. She pinned me with a stare that reflected on all I had said.

'Fuck it, yes. Absolutely yes!' she screamed before jumping into my arms. She winced, forgetting about the bruises that lay across her body, but I spun her around anyway, holding her tight. My heart felt full. Everything about her from the second I laid eyes on her, felt so right.

'Come, I'm feeling inspired.' I dragged her to my sculpting area. I had started carving a piece out of stone in my spare time. It was her: life-sized and made of soapstone. I chose this stone purposefully due to the softness of it. The morning after I met her, I ordered it in while I thought about how soft her skin had been under my fingers as I'd traced her body.

'I need to know your limits. How much do you want me to share in this collection? How vulnerable and exposed are you willing to be?'

She smiled, shaking her head. Her response was simple: 'Everything.'

Gently, I pulled the jumper she was wearing above her head, followed by her top. Her skin prickled at the sudden coolness of the air against her bare skin. Kneeling in front of her, I eased her pants down her legs, and she stepped out of them seductively. I had planned to tease her, but somehow she had turned it back on me. Standing, I slid my hand to her back, unclasping her purple bra and watching it fall to the ground. She stood there, bare, with nothing on but her black lace underwear.

Turning, I grabbed my Stanley knife from the nearest table. I slid the blade out slowly click by click. Her breath hitched as her chest rose and fell more quickly as I neared. I traced the back of it up her thigh before pulling the lace away from her skin, cutting through the fabric. I trailed the back of the blade against her stomach and down her hip, watching her shiver as she held her breath. The next cut sent the lace falling to the floor before I clicked the blade shut, dropping it to the floor.

The bruises on her skin looked darker today. More mottled. Anger flashed through me but I knew it wouldn't be long until I had my hands around the neck of the man that did this. I traced feather-light kisses over every bruise he left on her body and the scrapes on her hands. Her nipples pebbled and it took everything in me to walk away so I could take my place by the stone and look back at her. 'You're beautiful. So fucking beautiful it hurts sometimes.' Her cheeks flushed that beautiful colour that left my insides flipping to make it deeper.

She stood there facing me as I carved into the stone with my tools. She didn't pose; it wasn't a sensual piece. She knew, just as I did, that this was about power. Her unfiltered power. The hardness she bore to survive. It was raw and honest and required nothing more than for her to simply exist. We lost track of time, and it wasn't until the sunset and the studio darkened that I realised neither of us had moved for hours. I winced, realising she must be exhausted, but I was too enraptured to notice it until now. Putting my tools down, I looked at her—truly looked now, not with the analytical artist's eye I had been using. Now I was looking at her through the lens of a lover.

'I'm sorry, Sunshine. I didn't realise how long we had been going for—you must be exhausted and hungry.' Instead, I took in the flush of her cheeks and the tension in her body. *Oh.*

'Tell me, darling, how long have you been turned on for?' That flush deepened, and it made me want to sink my teeth into her.

'This whole time. The way you look at me. You look like you're gazing at a goddess, someone you worship. It made me feel wanted. Needed. Not to mention, you are so fucking sexy when you're working. The focus and concentration. I don't think I've ever seen anything more attractive than the way your hands worked over that piece.' I smirked at her confession.

'Sunshine. That's because I do worship you. I'm not sure if you realised this'—I stalked closer, pulling my dust-covered jumper over my head—'but you could ask anything of me. Tell me to lie down in the street and die; I would do it. Tell me to kneel and grovel at your feet; I would do it. Tell me to sign over every asset in my name to you while I stand there and watch you leave, and I would. I would stand at the door like an obedient little bitch waiting for her master to come home until my legs gave out. You own me, Sunshine. Mind, body and soul. I would do anything for you. You're in control of my heart, and you can either protect it or crush it. I would be grateful either way, knowing that you had touched it.'

Tears welled in her eyes as I placed my palm against her cheek, watching her sink into my touch.

'I love you,' she pushed out, trying not to crumble beneath the emotion that stirred within her at my confession.

'I love you too, Sunshine. Now, how can I offer you some relief?' I asked, trailing my fingers down her naked body. Her muscles tensed and her skin prickled. Her eyes closed, feeling the electricity of my touch on her skin.

I stopped waiting for her answer, holding my breath as the energy between us pulsed, her eyes locked on mine. Gone was the girl filled with doubt; here was a woman who stood in her own power.

'On your knees.'

*Fuck.* I sunk down, staring into her eyes the whole way. Unblinking. My hands wrapped around her thighs. I refused to break eye contact. I needed to watch her through this.

I licked up her slit and watched her eyes roll back as she bit down on her bottom lip. Her chest rising before she let out a ragged breath. Slowly, I did it again and again. I was rewarded with her fingers twining themselves into my hair as she pulled me harder against her as I focused on her clit. Sucking and licking, watching her watch me now. She wanted to fucking ride my face and it was everything.

I dipped my tongue inside of her, salivating at the taste of her wetness. I wanted more, so I dug deeper with my tongue as my face rubbed against her clit. I ate her like it was my last fucking meal and she rode me like that rung true. Grinding against my face, she took control of her own pleasure—using me like a toy—and it fucking did things to me. I dropped one of my hands between my legs, into my pants and glided over my own clit in time with the thrust of her hips against my tongue.

I could feel her building closer as her moans got louder and they turned into feral groans. I moaned against her—the feel of her losing herself on me, taking what she wanted, sent more pleasure through my body than my own fingers. My moan was her undoing.

'Look at me as I ride that pretty face of yours. Let me hear how much you love me using you.' I hadn't quite seen this side of her during sex before and it had my insides clenching with desire. I tried to look into her eyes but I was losing myself to the pleasure, and they kept shutting as I moaned at the feeling of my fingers, her delicious taste and the feel of her dripping down my face. I was close and as I dipped my tongue inside her, tasting the very depths of her, I let out a guttural groan that had her screaming. Gushing, squirting all over me. It sent me into a frenzy, lapping up the liquid before it could fall to the floor. I was a fucking animal for her as I found my own release; my body shuddered against her as my tongue slowed, but I kept licking, riding out the wave of pleasure as I savoured the taste of her.

'Wow,' she breathed.

'Wow,' I echoed. *Wow* was right. That was by far the best moment of my life. Being drenched in her want and need. I could throw away every dream I ever had for my life, including this gallery, because nothing else compared.

'What do you think?' I asked as I pulled her clothes back onto her body, being ever so gentle.

She stepped closer to the statue I had carved. It wasn't quite finished yet; it was rough and raw, but it still showed what I wanted it to. I had spent so much time on her eyes, the fierce flames that seemed to roil within them, that the rest being unfinished didn't matter.

'I wish I could always view myself through your eyes. I don't know if I deserve the way you look at me but right now it's what I need to see,' she said, stroking her fingers over the jagged stone.

'By the time I'm done with the collection, you will know every way I look at you. You will know your worth. You will see everything I see, and you will never doubt yourself or us again,' I promised, placing a kiss on her neck as I stepped into her.

'We should tell your brother. He's done so much for me. Do you think he'll be mad I don't want to work at the club or the store anymore? Oh my god, he paid for my online course and I'm just bailing on him.'

'I may or may not have texted him already. I was slightly too excited to wait. I told him to shove it and that I would be the one looking after you from now on, if you'd let me.' She paled and I couldn't help but laugh. 'Don't worry; he wasn't mad.' Pulling out my phone to reassure her, I showed her the text he'd sent.

Z: Good. Make her cry, I make you cry little sister.

She looked confused but relieved. My brothers' protective instincts over women were an enigma to many, but to me it made perfect sense. There had been a woman in his life once, when we were younger. This was before he became so hardened. She lived with us in the group home. She was only there for six months, and in that time, he fell hard. I suppose that trait ran in the family. They did everything together. One night, she was coming home late from a study group but never made it back. He had promised to pick her up but had fallen asleep.

He went looking for her when he woke and found her body stripped down, bloody and cold in an alleyway behind the library. She was dead. She'd been violated and killed by a group of drunk guys. He spent the next twelve months lurking in the shadows of their lives; tormenting them, driving them insane with fear, before he ended each one of them brutally. I didn't blame him then, but especially not now, because now I knew what it felt like to love someone. What I wanted to do to Jason after seeing the bruises on her perfect skin, rivaled what my brother had done to them. Losing her had changed him, turning him into something dark and twisted with a compulsion to protect those unlucky women who were alone in the world to make up for the one he felt he was responsible for losing.

'Sunshine, if you're ready, I need to know how many times Jason hurt you. I need to know how did he hurt you.' I turned her to face me as she put on the last of her clothing. Those endless brown eyes flashed with pain at wherever her mind took her. Her body shuddered, repulsed by the memories; it was different to how she shivered under my touch.

'Three hundred and seventy-one times. I remember every single one. He used his hands to beat me. A few times, he threw me into a bookcase or threw a cup or plate at me. He locked me in closets, handcuffed me to the radiator at times when his paranoia peaked.' My heart clenched.

'Did he...' I couldn't finish the sentence.

She looked at me, searching my eyes until it dawned on her. 'Once. He came home drunk and horny. It was one of the nights he had chained me to the radiator so I couldn't get away. You know what the worst part was? He had been gone for two days while I was locked there. He fucked me in a pool of my own piss. I-I had never felt so degraded in my entire life.'

I had no words, so I held her. I tried not to hurt her bruised flesh but I just needed to feel her so tightly against me until she was inside of me, shielded from the world and her past.

'V, I have something to ask you that I know I have no right to, but I think I need this.'

'Anything for you, Sunshine.'

'I need you to erase him—every touch, every memory. I need you to do the things he did to me: bind me, wake me with *you* being the one between my legs. Turn every terrible memory into something sweet and special because it's with you. Rebuild me.'

I swallowed thickly at what she was asking. It was a scary amount of trust she was giving me to reshape those memories. 'I'm scared of hurting you.'

'Would you stop if I asked you to?'

'Without a moments delay,' I replied instantly.

She grinned at me. 'See, you could never hurt me the way he did because he took from me. But here and now, I am deciding to give to you.'

'Okay, Sunshine, whatever you need. Now, I need to know if you want to be there. Xav will find him. Z will get him and Sunshine, I will make him feel every shred of pain and fear you felt with him until I kill him. The decision is yours: you can be there, you can be the one to do it, or you can choose to trust that I will make it hurt. Tell me what you want.'

She tensed briefly under me before the words left her. 'I want to be there at the end, after you've done what you wanted to him. I need to see him die. I need to know he can't find me again. That he's really gone.'

I nodded, promising her she would get exactly that.

'I also need to change my number; he found it somehow. I've been receiving text messages from him, V. He's been threatening me, telling me he'll find me. I'm getting scared. Really scared. What if he finds me here, and does something to you guys? The day he found me, he had left a note under the front door of the shop. I thought it was for the owner but it was too late when I had seen it, he said he would hurt you.'

My stomach dropped. I didn't think he would be able to get to her like that, but I should have known better, and I was angry at myself for not doing something about it sooner.

'How long has this been going on for, Sunshine?'

She shrugged, trying to deflate the anger she saw quickly brewing within me. 'This time? Only the last twenty-four hours or so.'

*God, how many times had this happened in the past? How*

*many times had she had to change her number or move because of him?*

If I wasn't certain before, I was now. I would kill him.

---

Later that night, once Sunshine was asleep, I called Ashleigh, Matt's wife. I had tried to leave them more or less undisturbed while on their honeymoon, but I desperately needed her advice now.

'Ash, I need your help.'

'Oh, my honeymoon's been great, thanks for asking V.' She mocked.

'Sorry Ash, I'm just freaking out right now. Tell me everything.'

'No, tell me what's going on, you sound off.' Her voice was tinged with confusion as I heard her close a door behind her, likely finding a private place for this conversation. It was rare I called her, we usually spoke via text or through Matt.

'I've met someone, and they're everything, Ash. I think I'm in love with her but she wants me to do something and...I don't know if I should or if I can.'

'Oh, hon I'm so happy for you. Now what's going on?' I know she wanted to pry more about this mystery person, as I had never previously shown much interest in anyone, and here I was seeking her advice about someone; but my desperate tone offered no room for pleasantries.

'She's gone through some of the same things you went through with an ex. She has a lot of bad memories. Ones she wants to erase. She's...she's given me consent to do things to her. Things he did. She wants me to replace all those bad memories with good ones, but I just don't know if it's the right thing to do. I also just don't know if I can tie her up or fuck her while she's unconscious knowing those were the things that sick fuck did to her.'

'Oh wow, yeah okay. Look at the end of the day only she knows what she needs to move past that trauma. Everybody processes things differently and if this is her way, then you need to put your own feelings aside and give her what she needs. And look this might help her, it might not. But at least she will know you will listen to her, you'll try anything to help her. Just know it will hit her randomly regardless—five years from now, without a trigger in sight, it will all come flooding back. Sometimes it's not so easy to fully escape it, but you can outrun it for a time. Help her in any way that you can and don't overthink it. Just be there however she needs you to be and give her the control. Show her, she's the one with all the power in this dynamic and she will always feel safe.'

Sighing, the tension left my body. I knew those words to be true, but I needed to hear them from someone else for them to truly sink in. The idea of ever taking control away from Sunshine the way he did made my blood run cold.

'Thanks, Ash. I don't know what I would do without you two.'

'Anytime. And V, cherish her. Truly cherish her.'

'I will. I got to go, give my best to Matt.'

'Will do but call him, he'll be mad knowing you called me and not him.' I laughed and hung up the phone. Letting out a tense breath I didn't know I had been holding on to, I exhaled deeply. I would be anything my Sunshine needed me to be.

---

'I have something for you.' I said pulling Sunshine onto the bed beside me. She looked at me with apprehension like all of this was too good to be true and she needed to be ready to run like she had her whole life, already churning through every worst-case scenario due to my serious tone. I watched the gears in her mind turn as she talked herself down from that edge and reminded herself, I'm not him, I'll never be him. To give me a chance and breathe though that instinct that pulled her into fight or flight.

'What is it?' she asked curiously but cautiously. Slowly I dragged the box that was lying on our bed closer lifting the lid. A small gasp left her lips. She didn't know how to react, I could see the hesitation.

'It's not for you. Well in a sense it is. I want you to use it on me.' Her eyes widened in shock.

'Um, I've never.' She said biting into her lower lip, eyes dropping back down to the black leather harness and matching dildo.

'I wanted you to know my words aren't empty. That I am wholly and completely yours. You own me Sunshine. You hold all the power. You hold all the control. So, let me submit to you.' Heat flushed up her neck as her eyes narrowed in on me. That worrying bite of her lip turned sharper as it morphed into one of arousal. She liked when I handed her the reigns and I made note to get on my knees for her every chance I could get.

She responded with a searing kiss, one that had pure desire throbbing between my legs. We clawed at one another pulling at our clothes until there was nothing left, each of us laid completely bare. She pulled back panting with need, my own breaths heavy as I took in her beautiful form.

Her eyes dropped down to the box but there was uncertainty swimming in them. It was an intimidating contraption all black leather and metal buckles.

'Here, let me.' I said kneeling on the ground before her as she stood above me like the absolute Goddess she was. As she stepped through, I dragged the harness up her supple legs, taking my time as I caressed her. A shiver raked up her spine. Once it was on and she got used to the feel of it, her demeanour completely changed. Hands on hips she looked down at me still kneeling at her feet. A mischievous amusement lit her eyes as a smirk laced her lips.

'Get me nice and wet for you.' She said throwing me the lube that had been sitting in the box. My insides clenched at the command. Her owning her power was quite possibly the sexiest thing I had ever seen and I would kneel before her until my knees were bloody if I got to catch a glimpse of her like this.

I did as I was told, coating her plastic cock with lube, never breaking eye contact. Her gaze heated my skin from the inside out.

'Get on all fours.' *Oh, Fuck.*

Scrambling onto the bed, I sunk down onto my elbows for her, arching my back and giving her a piece of me I had never given anyone. The delicate touch of her fingers as they trailed down to the tight ring of unused muscle had me flinching in anticipation. The cool liquid of the lube dripping on me and sliding down had me waiting on bated breath. A single finger nudged against me, lightly, easing against my hole. She pressed a little harder each time until I felt my muscle give way around her.

I sucked in a breath as pain lanced through me, and it wasn't the fun kind.

'Oh, fuck that hurts.' I ground out barely above a whisper, not wanting her to stop. But she either heard me or saw the tension in every muscle of my body. She leaned forward kissing up my spine until I felt her breath against my ear.

'I've got you baby. Relax for me.' She whispered as she kissed my temple and stroked my hair. I melted against her touch, our dynamic completely changing. I had been the one to take care of her through the raw emotional pain she had just been through but here she was supporting me though an acute physical pain.

I nodded once, still tense and not trusting my voice. I felt her push incrementally deeper. Bit by bit my hitched breathing eased. Once the pain turned to pleasure, she added another finger bringing back the pain but stretching me wider, getting me ready for her. She coated me in more lube as she added a third and final finger. Entering me in a steady rhythm that had me panting.

'That's it.' She said stroking my hair reassuringly. She twined her hand in my hair and began to pull. She waited to read my body language assessing if I was still there with her. Seeing what she needed to, she began pulling my hair back, instinctively I arched my back creating space as she slipped her fingers out of me. She hovered just outside of my entrance, the tip of her pressed against me.

'Now take it like the good fucking girl I know you can be for me.' She breathed into my ear before slamming into me. There was pain but so much pleasure as she pulled back out then drove home once more keeping a steady and firm pace. Not allowing me to take pause. I was immersed in her. Drowning in the sensations she was evoking with her hands and the snap of her hips. My moans built as did my pleasure the more I pushed through the sensations to take in the traces of her pleasure that seeped into the space around us. Her shallow pants, her nails digging into my hips, her hold on my hair tightening as she braced trying not to lose herself, the uneven rhythm of her hips as she got close to her own climax as the toy rubbed against her clit over and over again.

'You're *mine.*' She breathed as her grip tightened one more time, her hips faltering as she let out a low but rich moan that matched my own as she sunk into me deeper. Gone was the edge of pain this had started with, now it was pure pleasure, but it wasn't enough. She reached in front of me fingers finding my clit as she ground into me and rubbed her middle fingers against my clit over and over again. Up and down until my thighs jerked, muscles tensed and white exploded in my vision that radiated throughout my body. I slumped forward, limbs giving out.

Sunshine, pulled out of me, trailing her fingers over my back, laying sweet kisses between my shoulder blades.

'Thank you.' She breathed, tilting my head to the side so that I could face her as she laid down beside me.

'I should be the one thanking you, that was something else.' I said. She let out a light laugh.

'You know what I mean, thank you for giving me this. Giving me *you*. All of you.' Her soft supple lips pressed against mine, lingering there. Not forcing herself in, just basking in the moment and my presence. She took a deep inhale as she pulled back.

'You'll have all of me, always, Sunshine.'

# 11
# SUNSHINE

Weeks had passed since the De Luca's committed to finding Jason but there had been no updates. V's brothers said he had all but disappeared. It wasn't uncommon for him to go into hiding; he had some bad friends who he could hide with and who could cover his tracks. But I knew with the De Luca resources, his time on the run would be over soon. I still received the occasional threatening text from some new unknown number to remind me I wasn't rid of him just yet.

I agonised about what V planned to do with him once he was found. Not because I thought he deserved to live or that he was in any way redeemable. I agonised over it because of just how okay I was with the idea of his death. I had no hang ups, no guilty conscience, no conscience at all. Most normal people would at least struggle with the decision but I struggled with the wait until it was over. I *wanted* him dead. Perhaps I was a monster, but if I was, it's because he made me this way.

I quit my job at the Velvet Room and the art supply store, instead focusing my energy on my studies and helping V with her collection. I had never thoroughly enjoyed either line of work, but I cherished every moment with V and what we were creating together. Much of the help I gave her seemed to involve me posing naked for her, but I wasn't complaining. Soon enough, we fell into an easy rhythm together. I got used to family meals with the two men who no longer scared or intimidated me. Xavier, who was a stoic and quiet leader, was actually a bit of an awkward guy. Zane, beneath this brutality and violence, was just a giant lap dog.

I didn't feel like I was living with them, as V and I had an entire level to ourselves. She converted a spare bedroom into a study for me so that I could complete my course with minimal distractions. Really, it was just a room that I could lock, because anytime she was in my vicinity, she became a distraction, along with her wandering hands—not that I ever complained.

V had made significant progress on her collection. She was working on the final piece. Since the day I moved in, she seemed to be awash with inspiration and was constantly waking up to dash over to the studio in the middle of the night whenever something came to her. I was now less than a month away from finishing my course and had been planning the layout of the pieces in her gallery. She gave me complete control. It was exciting to use the things I had learnt and put them into practice for a collection as meaningful as this.

I padded upstairs after a long day of researching for my final assignment before my big exam. I was hungry and needed another dose of caffeine if I was going to wait up for V—her nights at the studio had been getting later and later recently. I had thought the communal level would be empty; it was rare for anyone to be home in the afternoon, but I found Zane pushing a stainless-steel trolley into the kitchen beside the marble island.

'V said you would be studying at a coffee shop today,' Zane said, halting in his tracks.

'Yeah, no, I changed my mind. I needed the quiet to focus. I can get out of your hair; I just came to grab something to eat.'

He shook his head and pulled out his phone; whatever he was going to do was interrupted.

'You ready, Z? I want to get this done before she comes back.' V strode into the kitchen, the rest of her words dying on her lips once she saw me. 'Sunshine? What are you doing here?'

'I could be asking the same of the two of you. Now, care to explain what you're hiding from me?' I crossed my arms and cocked a brow. Waiting.

'I was trying to warn you,' Z said, placing his phone back in his pocket.

I cleared my throat, dragging their attention back to me.

V looked at me and blushed. Actually blushed. 'Z was going to give me some new ink. I wanted it to be a surprise,' she said coyly averting her gaze.

V tripped while walking toward me, shattering the mug she had been holding.

Zane jumped up from his stool and yelled, 'Fuck!' before spinning to glare at V. It was his favourite mug.

Without meaning to, I flinched and stepped back. My hands shook as my breathing became shallower, my eyes darting between the siblings. I shrunk in on myself, Zane's reaction sending me back to the last time I had dropped something in front of Jason. I was placing a jar back in the fridge when my fingers slipped, causing the jar to shatter on the floor.

*'You stupid fucking bitch, can't you do anything right?!' Jason bellowed from the couch before deciding that wasn't enough. He stormed into the kitchen, rage wafting off of him, before slamming my back into the fridge. Dropping to the floor, I didn't dare groan in pain or cry out; that only made it worse.*

'Sunshine, hey Sunshine.' I heard V's distant voice pulling me from my memories.

Shaking it off, I turned to Zane. They knew what my reaction was, but I also knew they wouldn't press me.

'Hey lovely, come back to me. You're safe,' V said, placing a knife, handle first, into my hand. Blinking the daze away, I looked at it in confusion. 'If anyone does anything to make you feel cornered or threatened, use it. Even on us,' she said. It was beautiful and the handle had a little golden sun carved into the pommel.

'Sorry, Namazzi. I should have been more cautious about my volume and words around you. I would never lay a hand on you. I swear it,' Zane said, kneeling down in front of me, giving me control of the situation.

Raising the blade, I pointed it at his face. He grinned as I gripped the blade tightly before lowering it again. It made me feel stronger, even though everyone in the room knew they could overpower me in a fight in two and a half seconds flat—even without a weapon.

'I didn't realise Zane did your tattoos,' I said, breaking the tension after a couple of deep breaths.

Zane shrugged like it was no big deal and began to arrange his trolley. A cordless tattoo gun lay beside a pot of black ink, some Vaseline, paper towels and disinfectant spray.

'What were you going to get and where?' I asked, circling back to V, wanting it to be a surprise. I was intrigued.

'A single word: "Everything". I had planned to put in on my chest—over my heart. But now that you know, why don't you decide, Sunshine?'

I was floored. She wanted to brand herself with something that symbolised me, *us*. My heart beat with so many emotions that I could barely process them.

'I want one too,' was my only reply. Zane raised an eyebrow but V grinned. 'And you won't be hiding my mark under your clothes—I want it somewhere where everyone can see.' Zane rolled his eyes but the corner of his mouth twitched into the trace of a smile. 'I want it on the top of your right hand. I want you to see it all day, every time you write, pick up your phone or touch me. It'll be there.'

'Done, Sunshine. Z, you heard her. Let's do it.'

I was stunned for just a moment; it still shocked me at times how she just accepted anything I said, no questions asked. It was one thing to whisper sweet nothings about falling at my feet and doing anything to make me happy, it was another to actually do it.

V sat on the stool while Zane disinfected the marble bench. He took it seriously. This wasn't some garage-style stick and poke session after one too many drinks. It didn't take long for him to begin. V didn't flinch at the pain, which was no surprise considering she was covered in tattoos. She looked at me lazily, and before long, Zane was done.

It was a bold font—a strong choice that left no doubts. Lifting her hand, I marvelled at the pitch-black ink. Something in my heart clenched. I had never been claimed so wholly. No one had ever belonged to me so thoroughly that they would permanently mark themselves for me.

'Where do you want mine?' I asked.

Her tattooed hand fell away from mine as it trailed up my arm, caressed my shoulder and wrapped itself around the side of my neck. 'Right here, Sunshine—where I can feel your blood pumping for me. I want it just below your ear, trickling down your neck and ending just before the curve above your collarbone.'

I shivered but nodded in agreement, not trusting my voice, worried it would break as desire flooded through me.

Zane coughed, breaking the spell between us, amusement on his face as he shook his head. 'Let's get this over with before you start fucking and ruin my sanitary field.'

V held my hand tightly throughout my tattoo; the supple flesh of my neck made the tattoo gun feel as if it were slicing through my skin like a gaping wound. My mouth dried, and my body shook from the pain. I refused to stop. By the time the pain got too much and a single tear rolled down my face, Zane was pulling away having finished. V bent down to place a chaste kiss on my lips, sweeping my hair from my face and whispering praises into my ear that had my insides melting.

'Good girl.'

Those words had me losing myself. Forgetting Zane was in the room, I fisted her top, pulling her into me with such force that I fell off my stool, and as her body slammed into me, we went sprawling on the floor. Laughter burst through my chest, unable to contain the pure joy I felt radiating thorough me. Zane saw himself out without a word, but I could have sworn I heard him chuckle as he left.

The brothers would be working tonight which left V and me properly alone in this enormous house. We decided to snuggle up in the cinema room, and in poor taste, I picked out a classic mafia film called *Casino*. I couldn't believe V had never watched it. She cringed throughout the movie, talking about how unrealistic certain parts were and how her family would have dealt with the situation instead. I would have thought fear would lick up my spine but instead it was lust. Her fingers had nestled on my thigh under the blanket and she hadn't moved once. It was agony.

'Tell me something you've never told anyone, V. I want to know you better than anyone else ever has.'

She studied me for a moment, biting her bottom lip deciding on what to share.

'You know I don't work in the family business the way Xav and Z do. I've always had my own dreams and it's true—that is part of the reason. But there's another part of me, Sunshine—a deeper, darker shred of my soul that knows if I fell too deep into that world, I would lose myself. I'm just like them, and sometimes that scares me because what if I'm the worst of them both? My brothers said that, since I was a girl, I had this look in my eyes. It was never there for long but it was blood-curdling. I fear who I really am if I was to let go of my control. What I'm truly capable of. And it's not until I heard what Jason did to you that I truly understood why. It's bloodlust, Sunshine. I have a vindictive streak in me that makes me want to hurt those that hurt me or the ones I love a thousand times more than they could even dream.

'I keep my distance from the business as much as possible because if I didn't, I fear my reputation would be on par with Zane's in this city. It's always bubbling under the surface—the need to hurt someone, lash out and make them break—so I've spent my life channelling those emotions that have nowhere to go into my art. But seeing what Jason did to you. This is the first time I truly cannot suppress it. I don't even want to. I want to run toward this feeling and satisfy it. I just don't know if I'll be able to wholly find my way back to you after it, and that scares me.'

My hands squeezed hers tightly and reassuringly, because even after that confession, I still didn't fear her.

'Well, it's a good thing I fall into the category of people you love then,' I joked. She wasn't amused; concern rippled over her features as she glanced away.

'V, look at me.' I dragged her chin toward me. 'If this is a scratch you need to itch then do it. To be honest, it's something I need you to do. I know it's selfish, but I wouldn't feel sure or safe if it was anyone else ridding the world of Jason. But I will be there. I will be there for every moment, not just at the end. I will bear witness to it and I will pull you out if I see you drowning in it. I promise, you won't lose yourself. I won't lose you. I will not let that happen because I need you. *This* version of you with a touch of insanity. I've got you.' I was so sure of myself that the message seeped into her bones as her shoulders relaxed and her forehead met mine. I breathed her in as she did the same.

'How can you be so sure? How come you aren't afraid of me?' she asked, barely above a whisper.

'Because I know your heart, I know with every fibre of my being that you would never do anything to hurt me. Just the opposite. Because I am everything to you, you could never run from that or lose your way for long. You will always come back for me. For us. I know it in my bones, V. This isn't just love. This is cosmic. The universe, the gods—no thing or being would allow us to be a part.'

She let out an exhale before tilting her chin up and pressing her lips to mine.

'I am not scared of you. I could never be scared of you. You are my everything and I am well and truly yours,' I reassured her, kissing her temple, then her forehead, tracing down her nose, kissing her eyelids, her cheeks—every square inch of her face. Lightly, delicately. I was trying everything I could to reassure her that this connection went beyond our baser needs. I felt it in every fibre of my soul. I loved her; truly loved her. So those are the words I whispered to her as I placed chaste kisses all over her.

'I don't deserve you,' she whispered, more to herself than to me, but I heard it nonetheless. I gripped the hair at the back of her head and pulled, forcing her to look at me. Really look. She was shocked for a brief moment before the flash of pain turned into desire. I knew then exactly what she needed. She needed to know I could control her when she couldn't control herself.

'Follow me,' I demanded with a firmness in my voice that she hadn't yet heard as I turned leaving her without glancing back. I entered our bedroom and stood by the bed. A few seconds later, she was closing the door behind me. I raised my hand, making her pause by the door and preventing her from stepping forward. 'Take it all off.'

Her eyes flickered with desire. She pulled each piece of clothing off slowly, until she was left in a black lace bra and matching underwear.

'Your hand.' Her nostrils flared as she ripped off the bandage hiding her fresh tattoo. Slowly, she peeled the lace off her body, raising her brow in challenge.

'On your knees and crawl.' Turning my back to her, I walked the remaining feet to our bed and sat at the edge after pulling my own clothes off.

I watched her crawl; even with me above her on the floor, she looked like a predator stalking her prey. It almost drove me crazy. The heat in her eyes and the tension in her body. Ready to pounce. But I was in control this time. She stopped before me as I widened my legs in front of her. I had left my lace on, teasingly I dropped a finger and dragged it along my slit right over the lace. I loved the feel of it, I could imagine they were her fingers trailing over me, in public under a table somewhere.

She moved closer, licking her lips, ready to devour, but I wouldn't let her.

'Uh, uh. No touching me and no touching yourself. Watch and squirm.' I pushed my finger inside of me, feeling my wetness soaking the lace as I pushed it inside me, deeper. My head fell back as a breathy moan left my lips.

V's thighs rubbed together, her frustration building. I fingered myself a few more times, thoroughly soaking my underwear before sliding them off my hips.

'Open.' She went to spread her legs, thinking I was rewarding her for listening. How wrong she was. 'Your mouth,' I said.

Realisation hit her as she stuck out her tongue. I placed my scrunched-up, soaking wet panties in her mouth, but before I drew my fingers out, I pushed them deeper into the back of her throat. She made a gagging noise and clenched her fists but didn't move away.

Taking it.

'Good girl,' I purred as I lifted her chin, closing my panties inside of her mouth. I could see the heat in her eyes intensify as she tasted me on her tongue.

'Do you want me?' I asked, knowing she couldn't voice her response. I watched her stare at me intensely as she nodded her agreement.

'Would you do anything for me?' She nodded as I dragged my perfectly manicured toes up her thigh.

'Would you kill anyone for me?' She nodded as my toes trailed up her stomach.

'Would you stop anything you were doing and come to me if I needed you?' She nodded as I placed my foot on her bare chest and pushed her ever so slightly until she was sprawled out on her back.

'Spit them out.' She listened like the good little girl that she was. Total control coursed through me giving me a strength I was only just becoming familiar with.

She stayed there, unmoving, watching me as I stood over her. I hung my toes just over her lips. 'Will you always come back to me?' I asked.

She hesitated for a moment, her fears creeping in, before something settled over her: certainty. She nodded.

'Suck.' Her warm tongue enveloped my first toe and it sent shivers racketing up my spine. Her beneath me like this made me feel a power I had never felt before. She nipped at me playfully, but I pulled away; I was in control here, not her.

I walked away, leaving her on the floor and taking up my seat on the edge of the bed. I spread my legs, watching her gaze fall to the slit between my legs as she kneeled before me again.

'If you were trapped in the darkness, what would you do for a taste of me?' I asked as I slipped a finger inside of me, raising it to my lips before I sucked every bit of myself off of me.

'Everything,' she breathed.

'So, what do you have to fear when you have me?' I asked.

'Nothing.' She shook her head as if this one truth had quieted every fear screaming in her mind.

'Good girl. Now, come and eat.' I said as I spread myself wider.

She licked her lips as though she was about to feast on the finest food she had ever laid eyes on, like she had been starving before she plunged her tongue inside of me without warning. There was no preamble, just pure desperation and need. I felt her tongue deep inside me, as her face ground against my clit, sensations overwhelming me as one hand pulled my hips closer into her and the other found my breast, tugging at it, grabbing it like a life raft and she was drowning, drowning in me. My body fell back against the bed as I lost myself to the pleasure and feel of her body on mine, but I needed to make sure I erased every bit of doubt.

'What will you do when the bloodlust overwhelms you and you lose control?' I asked, pulling back and closing my legs. She let out a frustrated groan.

'What will you do when you can't control yourself?' I pushed harder as I pulled her onto me so that she straddled me.

She looked down at me, a depth that rivalled any look she had ever given me. 'I'll find you. I'll lose myself in you. I'll let you pull me back,' she said before she looked up at the ceiling, a single tear trailing down her cheek.

I traced a finger up, wiping it away. 'Good girl. I've always got you, V. Now lose yourself in me. Let every doubt and fear go. Give yourself fully to me. Brand yourself on my fucking soul and take me, in every possible way. I want everything you have to offer. This right here, right now, is my consent. Ruin me,' I pleaded as my hips ground under her, beckoning her touch.

Leaning forward she kissed me gently. Exploring my mouth with her tongue. 'I love you, Sunshine. You're everything I could want and everything I will ever need.'

Before I could respond, she slammed two fingers into me and watched as my back arched off the bed and my mouth popped open in a soundless gasp. As my eyes widened, her lips smirked at my undoing. This wouldn't be a fucking; this would be a claiming.

She pulled out her fingers, rubbing over my sensitive clit before delving back inside me, thrusting so deep I felt like she was searching for something and that's exactly when she found it. Her fingers curved inward and upward, brushing over that sweet spot inside me, sending a spasm throughout my entire body. I curled in on myself, overwhelmed, but she dragged her fingers out again giving me a sweet reprieve. Her other hand wrapped around my throat, forcing me to focus on her, and not allowing myself to be lost to the pleasure that shot through me. Her hand, gripping my throat, tightened as she slammed into me with her other fingers. She pushed and pulled, in and out of me, in the perfect rhythm, then faster—never once stuttering as my orgasm crested. Her grip on my throat tightened once more, so hard that my vision started to blur, but I held her gaze, showing her that I wasn't afraid of her dark side. That I knew she could never hurt me; she was only ever capable of giving me what I wanted, including that blissful balance between the two.

My nails dug into her skin until I felt the draw of blood under my fingers. My back arched as a scream forced its way out of me and her groans took on an animalistic edge. My body exploded with pleasure, and I kept screaming as she wrung out my pleasure. She kept that same pace with her fingers until I was sobbing, begging her to stop, but not being able to quite verbalise it because I could feel another wave coming—which I didn't think was possible—and I wanted to see how far she could push my body.

It was mere seconds until I was clutching at her, screaming once more. The black dots in my vision from the lack of air consumed me, and I passed out with V's sinister smirk being the last thing I saw. If I died like this, I would die happy.

I gradually woke up feeling a tickle between my thighs. I went to close them or swat away whatever it was but they barely moved until I felt them forced back as leather dug into my wrists and ankles. My eyes shot open and there was V, laying between my legs, lazily licking me, coaxing me awake.

'Where's the line, Sunshine? What can I do to you?' she asked as her hot breath shot thrills through my clit.

'Everything,' was my only response and all the permission and reconfirmation she needed to continue her exploration of my body and its limits.

She wasn't him. In one blissful moment she erased the memory of what he had done to me—tied to that radiator—and now this was the only way I ever wanted to be bound, like this, with her. We spent the next two days in bed as she fucked me to within an inch of my life, let me sleep, then fed me and fucked me again. By the end of it, I couldn't walk.

Every trace of Jason vanished from my body and my soul.

V carried me to her bathtub and climbed in, nestling me onto her thighs. I whimpered as her fingers trailed circles over my thighs. I knew what she wanted and I didn't know if my body could take anymore but yet I wanted it anyway. She hesitated, then stopped, and that made me angry for some unspeakable reason. I didn't want her to ever hold back from me. I wanted everything, always.

I slid my fingers behind my back and between her legs, catching her so off guard that she bucked in surprise under me. In the last two days, she didn't let me offer her any release; instead, she had gotten herself off while I climaxed when it got too much for her to bear.

Now that the claiming was over, it was time for me to seal the exchange.

My finger rubbed over her clit in slow circles with a firmness that had her hips chasing more. I threw my head back against her shoulder and breathed heavily in rhythm with the energy that pulsed between us, writing on top of her like I did that first night at the club.

'Fuck, Sunshine,' she gritted out.

I slid a single finger inside of her, going in easily thanks to the water. At this angle I couldn't thrust in and out of her, but as I slid out and palmed her clit I pushed another two fingers inside. Her gasp at the sudden fullness made my own legs tremble in desire.

I stroked my fingers inside her, curving them deeply, until she bucked again, telling me I had found it. My body writhed over her in time with the way I fucked her. Water sloshed around us and splashed onto the tiles but I just went harder and faster.

Her breathing grew ragged as she gripped the edge of the tub, holding back. Always holding back, trying to be in control.

Pulling her hand off, I dragged it down my breast, squeezing before I pushed it between my legs and pushed her fingers inside of me.

She matched my rhythm as she plunged inside of me, staying there with three of her own fingers. She matched my strokes and it wasn't long until our pants turned into moans and I was having to grip the tub with my own free hand. This was everything—the moment we both lost ourselves to each other. The separation between us dissolved in the water as our bodies turned into one writhing mess. We were an extension of each other as every muscle, breath and stroke moved in unison—so did our screams.

# 12
## VALENTINA

Xavier sat across from me. 'We've found him. He's spent the last few weeks jumping from state to state but he's back in town now. It's only a matter of hours until our people can pinpoint his location. We weren't able to track him as the Russians were helping to cover his tracks for a minute there. But it seems Jason has a gift for pissing people off and their protection quickly ran out.'

Finally, we had been searching for weeks, and although my girl knew she was safe with us, I could see the flicker of fear every time we told her we hadn't made any progress in our search for him.

'Go and get ready for the opening. You've both put a lot of effort into tonight. I'm proud of you little sister,' Xav said, getting up from behind his desk and giving me a hug and kiss on the forehead.

Z stepped forward then. 'As soon as we have a location, I'll grab him and take him to the desert. I don't want you worrying about a thing. This is your night.'

I got ready, wearing a gold satin suit that my little Sunshine had handpicked. She had chosen a floor-length, body-hugging gown in a similar fabric. She looked incredible as she strode down the stairs. She was everything. I loved the way she looked at me when her eyes landed on what I was wearing. They lit up with excitement; there was a pure, innocent joy that I had feared was lost forever, but slowly, through me, she was coming back into her own. This was my purpose. This was why I had made her such an integral part of every facet of my world. I wanted the good things to seep into her and warm the cold, broken bits, mending them. I wanted her to finally have hope for a better life, and in this moment, for the first time, she was basking in it, knowing wholeheartedly that she deserved every good thing that had come from our time together. She was letting go of her past, her pain, and her fear.

The show would be starting in a matter of hours. Sunshine had worked around the clock to arrange my pieces, telling the perfect story of our love and lust. Hundreds were expected to be in attendance; my girl had done an incredible job with the promotions over the last few weeks. Many wanted to come and see if a De Luca was even capable of creating rather than destroying, but it only fuelled our desire to prove everyone wrong.

The final piece in the show was still a secret, and one I had not shown to anyone yet, not even my girl. It had been a point of contention between Sunshine and me—this was just as much a part of her show as it was mine—but I gave her some nonsense about it being part of my process and, ever the dutiful muse, she begrudgingly let it go. She did not know that this piece was performative and required her to be in the dark.

'Sunshine, you look fucking ethereal. I cannot thank you enough for everything you have done. If it wasn't for you, my dream would never have become a reality. I love you.' She blushed as her hands slid up the satin collar of my blazer, wrapping around me. Warm lips crashed into mine, trying to claim me in the threshold of our home before we left our little safe space and finally told the world who we were and what we were. Everything. That is what we named the show—how fitting.

I held the door for my girl as she strode past, casting a seductive look over her shoulder, enticing me. She would drive me crazy all night until I kicked every last guest out of my gallery just to spend a moment alone with her. This was her revenge for me hiding the final piece. As her hips swung from side to side with each step, I had to bite down on my knuckles to stifle a moan. She was ravishing as the silky gown flowed over her form like incandescent water.

The car ride over did not get any easier as her slender fingers trailed my thigh in little circles, edging closer but never quite close enough. I gripped the steering wheel for dear life the whole drive over, as I was seconds from pulling over and saying *fuck it* to the biggest night of our lives, just so I could have a taste of her.

We arrived a couple hours earlier than our guests, wanting to ensure everything was perfect for them. Parking behind the gallery, we took the back entrance. Soon, the place would be bustling with waiters and caterers, but for now, it was just for us to bask in the glow of this monumental moment and the tireless effort we had put in.

Flicking the lights on, horror flooded my veins as my sweet little Sunshine screamed. Stumbling further, she tripped on her heels. I grabbed her as she clutched my arm, taking in the scene that lay in front of us. Every piece was shattered, destroyed and drenched in red paint. The paintings had been slashed. Nothing was left whole. Everything had been turned to dust, just like that. My favourite painting, the one that had started it all, was the only one that was left whole, but it was no better off. In big black letters, the words *SHE'S MINE* were sprayed in paint.

Sunshine dropped to the floor, sobbing and pulling at the broken pieces of my sculptures that lay in the rubble at her feet. The strangest part was that I didn't care about the show as much as I thought I would. What tore me to fucking pieces was seeing my girl crumble amongst the wreckage. She had put so much into tonight and it represented so much more than us and our short but intense journey. It was a fresh start for her. The beginning of a new life, a new her.

I shot a quick message to my brothers, knowing exactly who did this.

'It was Jason, it had to be,' she breathed, looking up at me from the floor, tears cascading down her face. 'I'm so sorry.'

My heart clenched at the sight. 'It's not your fault, Sunshine. None of it is your fault. It will be okay; besides, there's one piece he couldn't get his hands on.'

She sobbed harder, inconsolable and feeling responsible. Knowing that words were of no use right now, I held her, letting the warmth and softness of her skin envelop me, stilling my own pounding heart.

She always calmed me, no matter what; and as that familiar bloodlust roared in my ears, I clung to her, my grip bruising but unable to let go. Because if I did, there would be no stopping me. Once again, he took something from her. Soon, my fingers turned numb, and I didn't even know where I was holding her—only that she was safe in my arms. Thank every god he only managed to get his hands on our collection and not her; though I would be cursing my brothers for not seeing this coming with all the eyes they had out searching for him.

'Interrupting something am I?' came a deep voice from the hallway that led upstairs to my studio.

Sunshine let out a quick gasp and clenched me tighter. My eyes landed on him as he walked out of the dark cover of the wall and approached, gun pointed directly at us.

Slowly peeling her hands away from me, I stood up and stepped between the gun and my girl. 'Just a little bit. Now, if you don't mind, we have a bit of cleaning up to do.'

A bark of laughter was his only response before the rushing of footsteps and the cold press of a barrel met me. 'This isn't a joke, bitch.'

'I didn't think it was. Now if you don't mind, I need you to fuck right off. You're scaring my girl and you've already pushed me further than you want to.'

He pushed the barrel of the gun harder against my forehead breathing hard he almost spat with rage at the notion I didn't fear him. I assumed his default was that women feared him, and this was quite an unusual turn of events for him.

I looked past the rage, the scruffy jawline and slightly shaggy hair. He was handsome enough, with nice blue eyes and a decent build, but I still couldn't see it. My girl with him. Even cleaned up, he wasn't even close to her level, but I supposed he knew that; those insecurities driving his need to control her.

'Namazzi, it's time for you to come home with me. You had your fun; now let's go. There's nothing left for you here. Come home with me. Where you belong.'

She stood, gripping the back of my blazer before finding her voice, embodying the once whole sculpture that now lay broken at her feet. She was like a phoenix rising from the ashes.

'No. Fuck no,' she spat.

Jason's face flushed with anger and sweat. He looked high out of his mind. 'I suppose there's one thing left for you here, but I can end that quick enough.' He cocked the gun, ready to shoot, and as if anticipating his response, Sunshine pushed me out of the way.

*Bang.*

A scream escaped me, fearing the worst that she had taken the bullet meant for me as the sound rung out, bursting all rational thought and leaving ringing confusion swirling in my mind. Blood was seeped into her gown. But the shot didn't come from his gun and the blood wasn't hers.

Z stood a few feet away, a quiet, brutal anger lacing his features. Cool hands pulled me into a hug. Jason lay groaning on the floor but it was Sunshine's panicked words that I heard.

'Are you okay? Are you? I'm so sorry, baby. I'm so sorry. This is all my fault. I love you, please tell me you're okay.' She was spiralling. Pulling back my hands, I caressed her cheeks lightly before firmly gripping her face, snapping her attention to me.

'I'm fine, thanks to you. None of this is your fault, Sunshine. It's ours. Z should have found his arse a lot sooner.' Z grunted in the back, angrily agreeing.

She shook her head, about to argue once more, but I crashed my lips to hers, warmth coating my tongue as my arms wrapped around her, pouring all my gratitude that she was safe into that moment. Jason groaned in pain, dragging us back to reality.

'Z, you know where to take him, but be back in time for the show.'

'What show? Everything is ruined.'

'No Sunshine, *everything* is right here.' I said stroking her cheek, gazing into those endless brown eyes.

We didn't pay much attention to her ex's body being dragged from the space, as our eyes were locked on one another. Too scared to look away in case we slipped through each other's fingers. That was far too close a call for my liking.

She finally looked away from me, taking the extent of the damage all in, her shoulders caving under the weight of it all.

'This show is our story, including the ugly. Let's show them how perfection can drive an insecure man mad. How perfection can survive the unimaginable and still rise. How perfection bends but doesn't break. *You* are perfection. You go and get ready for the caterers and the guests. Get yourself cleaned up and find us some new clothes. I'll worry about the art.'

She hesitated but nodded, heeding my instructions. I knew exactly what to do about this.

# 13
# SUNSHINE

I had no idea what V was going to do to fix this. I didn't think the night was salvageable unless she had a whole second collection hidden away somewhere, but I trusted her. I trusted her more than I trusted myself or anyone who had ever entered my life. On the way back home, I wondered when it had become my home; yet somehow, that's exactly what it was. I called the caterers, waiters and other vendors to explain that there had been a break in, but they were still supposed to carry on as rehearsed. In the meantime, I rushed back home to find new clothes. It was the first time in a long while that I felt comfortable being by myself, but knowing Jason was with Zane, I had nothing to fear. He had already tried his best and failed.

The house was oddly quiet after the commotion of this afternoon, but it didn't take long to find some clean clothes for the pair of us. Sliding out of my blood-soaked satin gown I pulled on one of V's power suits, red like the lingerie I wore the first night I met her and fitted in all of the right places. I pulled out a second one for V; this time, it was white. She had darkness lurking within her, but in my chaotic life, she was a bright light of hope.

It wasn't long before I was back on the road, heading to the gallery. I found V taping ripped paintings back together. Some of the broken sculptures had been slightly repaired and glued together, but they were still half crumbling.

'Step back, Sunshine. I can't have you ruining your clean clothes.'

I quirked a brow, not understanding what was coming, but then I saw it. A large paint pot of blood-red paint. She poured it over the broken edges of the sculptures and painted it across the gashes in the paintings she had pieced together. She streaked paint across the ground from each piece she had, which now looked as though they were bleeding onto the floor, culminating in a giant pool of blood. What no one else would know is that Jason's blood lay there, mingling with the red paint. In the center sat a silver serving tray with a lid on top.

'What do you think?' she asked.

My eyes lingered on the serving platter. Was this some joke about how she would be serving Jason's death to him by the end of the night?

'I think it's slightly more morbid than we had initially planned and that you need to change. The catering staff is nearly done and visitors will be arriving shortly.'

She smiled at my obvious, creeping anxiety. 'It will be okay; trust me,' she reassured me, taking the bag of clothes from my hand before placing a chaste kiss on my forehead.

None of this is what I had envisioned for our first show, but I knew it would work out. Nothing in my life ever had, but here with her, it was a certainty.

The first visitors began to arrive while V was getting

dressed after a quick shower in the bathroom upstairs. Waitstaff with wine circled the room as finger food made its way around.

Xav was the first of V's brothers to arrive. I didn't know how to approach him in public, let alone after all that had happened. I felt seconds away from losing my mind without V next to me to ground me.

'Namazzi, it looks incredible,' Xav said. 'Not the show I was expecting, but V has always had a talent for pulling beauty from chaos. I suppose that's how she found you. This collection, it makes more sense now than the snippets I saw before.'

I was slightly too stunned to speak, but before I could find the words, V stepped into the room, and she was glowing. The atmosphere in the room lightened as she strode in, eyes darting to her, with everyone wanting to approach her, but her focus was single minded. She came to me first where I was ushering in the visitors. She placed a gentle kiss behind my ear before turning to her brother.

'Update,' she demanded, not bothering with pleasantries.

Xavier stifled a smile but indulged her. 'Z is on his way back. He has an IV drip keeping him unconscious; should he wake, he is chained down, and no one would be able to hear him isolated in the desert.'

'Good, and the police?'

Fear gripped me. *What police?*

I gripped V's arm, but she squeezed me back reassuringly.

Xavier jumped in quickly before my mind ran away from me. 'The police on duty when the gunshots went off are in our pocket. No one called in the sound; there's construction on the other side of the block so it would be easy to think it was coming from there.'

I exhaled, releasing tension I did not know I was holding on to.

'Thanks, Xav. Will you be there tonight?' she asked.

'Of course. For now, enjoy all of this and we will do what comes next together.' With that, he took a glass of champagne as a waiter walked past and folded into the crowd to examine the pieces more thoughtfully.

We greeted the visitors as they came in; some were there for me, from my college classes, including my professor. This was the first time I had met any of them in person, as all my classes had been online, but I was shocked they had made the effort. V held my hand through it all, unable to let go of me given everything that had happened.

'So, this is the woman who has had you hidden away, V? I can see why you forgot about me now. So much for *nothing and no one*.' A familiar face that I couldn't quite place stepped forward, embracing V in a hug that had me riling with a touch of jealousy.

'I remember you!' he exclaimed, pulling me in for a far too familiar hug. 'You work at the Velvet Room. How on earth did you lock her down, V?' The bucks party, the night I had met V—he was the groom.

'Worked. She's my gallery director now, and I wasn't hiding her; it was you who chose to go on a two-month-long honeymoon across Europe and it was also you who got married first so shove your nothing and no one, we aren't kids anymore. Besides, I didn't want to disturb your happy little bubble. Is the wife here?' V asked.

Matt laughed, seeming unphased by her bluntness. I had heard a lot about him and their friendship. He was like another brother who had been there for her through the social isolation being a De Luca brought, one of the few who didn't fear her family and its name. The tension in my body faded as I took in the warmth with which he looked at V.

'You know Ash; she's working late—doctors and their ridiculous schedules. So, what's your lovely lady's name?'

'Namazzi,' I replied.

Matt quickly ushered me away, ignoring my protests as well as V's and the fact that I was working, instead pulling me into a corner and thrusting a glass of champagne into my hand.

'Now, here comes the obligatory threatening speech. Her brothers won't openly say this because their faces alone will strike the fear of God into anyone sane, but I will. Don't hurt her. Please. You can't hurt her. She's been through too much, been abandoned one too many times. I've never seen her with anyone, at least not seriously, and I need to know that you're serious about her too. If you hurt her—'

'If you hurt her, what Matt? Are you threatening a member of the family?' Zane stepped forward, crowding over Matt.

'I was just setting the ground rules. Looking out for V is all.' He looked sheepish and slightly intimidated.

'It's okay, Zane; it was far from scary. If anything, it was touching and slightly amusing.'

Matt looked between us in disbelief as Zane's admission of my being family sunk in.

'You are serious, thank fuck!' Matt clasped me around the shoulder, grinning and shaking his head. 'Why didn't you just say so? You had me looking like a fool, trying to play the macho big brother act.'

'V said you could be overzealous at times and just to roll with it, so I wanted to see what she meant; it didn't disappoint. Besides, I'm sure of her you know. I won't hurt her. She's mine just as much as I'm hers.'

'You know she's going to marry you, don't you? If you're here, you're part of the family. She's not letting you go.'

'Here's hoping.' I grinned.

The gentle clink of cutlery against a wine glass rung out in the gallery, and conversations halted as people gathered toward the center of the room. There V stood before the pool of red paint at her feet. She held out a hand, gesturing for me to step forward and take my place as the director of this show.

'Thank you all for coming. This collection means a lot to the two of us,' I said, stepping into the crook of V's arm. 'As you walk through these walls, you will see how love changes the soul and how it changed me. Everything in me was surface level, but it was Valentina who brought my strength, confidence and hope to the surface. As you step through, you will see the weight of the past dragging us back, trying to intervene in something that was destined. But here we stand, together as one. Even as the wounds of the past try to pull us apart and bleed into our present, we still remain everything to one another,' I finished.

V looked at me with such admiration that I barely registered her talking for a moment so swept up in her eyes.

'When you find your everything, you hold onto it with both hands. Even if everything falls apart around you, as long as you have each other, you will find beauty in the darkness.'

She bent down to the silver platter that lay in a mixture of blood and red paint and pulled off the lid. There lay a red velvet box. V picked it up carefully, opening it as she sunk her white satin knee into the blood before me.

'Sunshine, you are everything. Without you, I am nothing. Let me hold onto you with both hands and be that ray of light that pulls me from the grime and darkness of this life.'

Tears dripped down my cheeks as I sunk to the floor with V. We were reborn, starting something new and beautiful from the ashes of something old and broken. I slammed into her, our lips colliding as we fought to hold on to each other, not drowning in the darkness that lay at the edge of the night. This moment being our north star to one another always.

At some point, V pushed the ring onto my finger, but by the time we were done, we were a mess of red paint and blood smeared over our limbs and faces. Right back to how we looked at the start of the night. The crowd cheered and soon we were enveloped by Matt for a hug as he whispered *I told you so* in my ear. Xavier hugged his sister in a way I had never seen from the cold and detached man before, warmly. Zane pressed his forehead to hers and whispered something to her that made her punch his arm as he laughed. I had never seen her brothers so at ease, defences down and filled with joy—joy for their little sister. For *us*.

Xavier and Zane turned to me, each hugging me kindly; it was the first time either had dared to lay any kind of hand on me aside from the tattoo that laced my neck. I had always thought my skin would crawl under their touch, as scary as they were, but it was comforting in a way I had only ever felt from V—my family. That's who they are now. They welcomed me from the first day, fought for me, and even helped more than I ever expected them to with Jason.

The rest of the evening went off without a hitch. We

made the rounds, and I spoke to a few journalists and critics. Many were impressed by the spin and the performance art nature of the proposal to tie the show together. Many promised glowing reviews, and it sent a pang of pride through me. My girl was incredible, and soon everyone would know it. Not just her name, but her talent.

# 14
# VALENTINA

It was late by the time we wrapped things up at the gallery. My little Sunshine had fallen asleep in the car as Z drove us to our desert safe house. Xav had left earlier to keep an eye on Jason, having seen him stir ever so slightly on the cameras after partially knocking out his sedative-filled IV line.

On the outside, it looked like a decrepit wooden shack of a home, with broken windows and creaking hinges on the doors—not unlike one of the homes where we had found ourselves hiding as children. In the laundry, there was a secret door at the back of the linen cupboard. It opened to a winding staircase that went three levels below. Sunshine didn't react, but I could hear her little gasp as she took in the thick concrete walls and the reinforced door that sealed shut as we descended. It was a fortress; there was no coming in or out, and not a lick of sound would penetrate through. We could do what we wanted down here, and no one would ever know.

Zane led the way until we reached the landing on the very last floor. Xav sat in a chair smoking a cigarette as

Jason sat across from him, chained to his. Cigarette butts littered his thigh, where Xav had undoubtedly been extinguishing his last hour of chain smoking. A tinge of burnt flesh greeted my nostrils, along with the smell of piss. Looking at Jason's jeans, it was easy to see why.

'Sunshine, do you want any part in this?' I asked, stepping in front of her and pressing my forehead to hers. Breathing in her scent and holding on like hell to this moment and to her, as I felt the red-hot rage burning under my skin, clawing at me to eviscerate the man that had hurt her. Her bruises had faded, but the scars on her heart would remain for years to come, and I would make him pay for it all.

'His last breath. It's mine,' she said as her lips found mine. Pulling back, she whispered, 'Thank you.'

I pressed my lips to the tattoo on her neck then lifted her left hand.

'It's beautiful,' she said, and it was. I kissed her hand as the emerald-cut ruby glinted against the fluorescent lights. It matched the red she wore the night I met her, while the yellow gold band shone like sunshine against her deep skin, looking perfect on her slender finger.

Xav stood, offering his seat to my girl. Taking it further away, creating as much distance between her and the man that had haunted her, she nodded her appreciation to my brother. He stood next to her, guarding her as he would for me.

Z dragged a stainless-steel table laden with tools, knives and other more creatively painful contraptions. 'Need some help sister?' he asked, grinning. These moments were the happiest I had ever seen Z. On the cusp of or immersed in bloodshed was where he belonged. It's what I feared to be, I looked at Sunshine once more, my grounding force. Promising not to lose myself here and now.

'I need to do this brother but thank you. Both of you,' I said, clasping the back of his neck as our foreheads met. I was closest to Z because we were so much closer in age with him only being three years older and we had an unspoken understanding, recognising the truth of who we were at our depths, even if I kept mine leashed. Two sides of the same fucked up coin.

Grabbing the smelling salts, I ripped the IV out from Jason's arm and held them under his nose until he was retching himself awake. His eyes snapped open, and slowly he took in the room and its inhabitants before him. Fear glinted in his eyes as they landed on Z, but tonight Z would be the least of his fears because he had awakened something in me that needed to be released.

His mouth opened as if to ask *Why?* before his eyes settled on my Sunshine. She sat there poised, unflinching, with a strength I hadn't yet seen radiating from her. This is what I had always wanted to see—my girl without fear, surrounded by her new family.

'Do not look at her. Do not speak to her. Your problem lies with me.'

His head swung back to me, the tone of my voice stoking something within him. Fear.

'I have no issues with you. My issues are with that whore over there.'

*CRACK*. His head whipped back so hard I thought for a moment it would sever his spine as my fist landed on his cheek.

'Lay your hands on what's mine, and I assure you, she is mine,' I said, holding up my own matching ruby-and-gold ring for him to see. 'Do that, and your problems with her become solely my problem.' Blood dribbled from his lip; the impact of the hit was immediate. I was slight, but I had been training my whole life with my brothers. It's why I had never needed a bodyguard even with the amount of people my brothers had pissed off.

'She's... mine. Always will be. I've tainted her so thoroughly there's no getting rid of me,' he spat, blood landing onto my already-stained white suit. I laughed—genuinely laughed—at his arrogance.

'She stopped being yours a long time ago. You may have had her body for a time and even her fear, but her mind and soul, they were never yours. Your dirty hands never scratched the surface. And believe me when I say, you are well on your way to being erased—so completely that she will forget your name, your face and your disgusting touch. The first step is erasing you.' I stepped towards the table, caressing everything that lay there, ready to be used. My fingers settled on a cold sharp blade. One edge smooth; the other serrated.

Stepping into Jason's space, I dragged the fine tip up and over his arm, which was chained to the armrest. Once I got to his shoulder I sank the smooth edge into his skin and dragged it back down slicing a cut all the way down to his wrist. He thrashed against his chains and yelled out in pain, calling me every expletive there was.

'Bit of an overreaction, Jason. I'm only just getting started. I'm going to make you fear me the way she feared you.' I did the same to his other arm and watched his blood pool onto the floor. Slamming the blade into the middle of his hand, I pinned it to the armrest and he let out a blood-curdling scream. Ignoring him, I stalked back to the table to get the barbed wire.

I wrapped the barbed wire against his throat so tightly

he could barely breathe let alone swallow. It was agony. 'So many times she begged, pleaded and screamed for you to stop until her throat was raw. It's time for you to have a little taste of what that might have been like.'

Casting a glance at my girl, she looked at me—not Jason, never at him. She was here for me, and I didn't see fear or disgust in her eyes. I saw love. Grabbing a set of pliers, I knelt on the floor in front of him, watching the sweat drip from his clammy brow.

'Every finger that touched her is mine now.' Closing the pliers over his fingers, I twisted and pulled, then twisted again as I pushed against the bolted-down chair with all of my weight until it ripped from his body. Dropping the finger, I moved to the next as his thrashing screams turned into defeated sobs, unable to comprehend the pain. After I had ripped every finger off his left hand, I pulled the blade from his hand and used the serrated edge to saw through the fingers on his right hand; one by one they dropped to the floor. There was so much blood. I scooped some up from the floor and held it to his lips, forcing it down his throat watching him choke on it.

'Z, unchain him.'

But before he could move Xav interjected. 'He should stay tied down, V.'

Walking over to my brother, I pulled his gun from his hand and shot Jason in each foot. The screams broke as they forced themselves up his throat.

'There, he's not going to be able to do anything without any working hands or feet.'

Z, the sick fuck, laughed. 'She's got you there, brother.'

As Z unchained him, I grabbed a metal clamp and an even larger knife this time. Jason's heavy panting only made the wire around his neck dig in more. Blood dripped from where the spikes had embedded themselves into his flesh every time he screamed. I slashed at his belt, not bothering to be careful. 'I never thought I would be undressing a man ever again.' I laughed.

'And you never will,' Sunshine spoke, steel in her voice as her eyes seared into mine, jealousy rearing its head in her and igniting something sadistic in me.

'You took her against her will, Jason, so now I'm going to take something precious of yours.' Clamping down on his below-average dick, I hacked into it at the base. No sound left him—the pain too immense—as he gaped at me and what I had done. Not giving him a single moment of reprieve, I pulled him from the chair until he was sprawled on his stomach. The tip of my blade caressing his cheeks until I poked the tip into his arsehole. Jason's body spasmed under the pressure. Slowly, I pressed harder as I cut his hole wider.

Unintelligible begging escaped from him. 'Do you fear what I can do to you now, Jason?' A barely coherent, affirmative sound escaped him. 'I would ask if you're sorry, remorseful for what you did to her, but I know what your answer would be and how much of it is just self-preservation at this point. 'Can you imagine what it would have been like to be violated by you? Well, no need to imagine it. You can feel it.' With that, I slammed the metal clamp holding his cut-off member and plunged it into his bleeding arsehole. Leaving it in there, clamp and all.

'Sunshine. Come,' I breathed, outstretching my hand for her.

Without hesitation, she stood, stepping into me. We pressed against each other, foreheads meeting, breathing one another in as her abuser lay on the floor, incoherently sobbing in his own blood.

'Are you ready?'

She nodded, pressing her lips to mine. I gave her Xav's gun and kicked Jason's body over so that he laid on his back, staring up at her. She stood over him, raising the barrel to his head with a stillness and surety that I wasn't expecting.

'You will never hurt me again.' And with that, a single gunshot rang out, followed by another and another, until all the was left was the sound of her clicking an empty gun. She drained every last bullet into his head until his face was unrecognisable. A second later, she was vomiting all over his dead body. I patted her back in soothing circles, whispering how she was such a good girl. *My good girl, not his—never his.*

Wiping her face on my sleeve, she straightened herself, looked at me and said the words that would finally free her. 'It's over.'

# 15
# SUNSHINE

The following week was a blur. We decided to close the exhibit after its first night; however, that seemed to generate even more interest online, and we had people contacting us nonstop for private viewings, offering exorbitant amounts of money for fragments of rubble from the destroyed sculptures.

I had assumed that killing a man would rattle me more, change me and shake me down to my core, but I was fine. We came home, stood under a steaming hot shower and then went to bed where V worshipped my body until the sun rose. She called me her good girl and told me how proud she was of me, over and over again. She never needed to fear losing herself because she never lost me. We didn't leave her bedroom for three days straight as we fucked each other raw, breaking ourselves down to our baser components and rebuilding each other back up to who we needed and wanted to be. Not the monsters we were in that basement.

Tonight would mark us finally starting over, so we made our way to the Velvet Room where all of this began—

except tonight, I wouldn't be dancing for anyone besides V. We had booked out that same private VIP room where I had ground myself against her to the point where I had come on her thigh all those months ago.

Closing the door behind us, I locked it. V made her way to the large sofa, sinking down into the middle of it. She wore a black leather skirt and an emerald-green velvet top. Her tattoos were on full display, complemented by a fresh set of stiletto-shaped nails that matched the shoes on her feet.

A shiver went up my spine as I pictured them raking over my skin. My eyes met V's, and that same hungry look in her eyes that had captivated mine from that first night was there. They burned into my soul—snaring me, claiming me, wanting me.

Slowly, I stepped closer to her, swaying my hips in time with the music, pushing the straps of my slinky black satin dress—which hugged my skin—down to the ground. I followed the clothing to the floor, stalking on all fours towards her, with an arch in my back and a heavy-lidded gaze. I threw my head to the side as I came up to her ankle and did what I wanted to do that first night but couldn't. I licked her all the way from her ankle to her thigh, biting down on the soft flesh just under her skirt. She shook under my touch as pleasure mingled with pain.

In time with the music, I gripped her thighs, pushing them apart so I could drag my lace-clad body upwards until her face buried itself in my breasts. This time she could touch me. Taking a lace-covered nipple into her mouth, she drew a moan from me. Pulling her head back by her hair, my tongue landed at the base of her throat as I dragged it up her neck. My teeth grazed over her ear as a loud crack landed on my arse cheek. I moaned again and swung my hips over her—need taking over my movements—searching for her, for relief.

She dropped onto her back and pulled me up her body until I hovered over her, pulling my lace to the side as she slammed me onto her face, devouring me—sucking and licking like she hadn't had a drop of water for days. I could hear how wet I was as her tongue drove itself inside me, then back to circle my clit. I writhed on top of her and as I threw my head back to moan, another slap landed on my arse cheek. A warning.

*Look at me*, her eyes said. That same grin she always evoked in me appeared on my lips. She snaked a hand up my stomach, over my breast, and gripped the tattoo that lay on my neck. Everything between us had started from this place; right here and right now, I was living every fantasy I'd had in these walls from the moment I met her.

Her tongue moved quicker as she sucked on my clit. My body tensed, climbing after the pleasure she gave me. Soon enough my hips stopped writhing and turned into grinding—over her tongue—finding that pressure that sent spikes of pleasure so intense. My moans turned primal as I stared into those eyes. I hadn't realised her other hand was in between her legs, chasing her own release, until the vibrations of her moans shattered me completely. Screaming out in pleasure, she enveloped me in her mouth and sucked, squeezing every last bit of pleasure and drop of wetness from me as she let out her own muffled scream.

I sat on her for another minute as she caught her breath. She wasn't ready to let me go—slowly lapping at my cunt, wanting to savour the taste. All it did was start me up again, wanting more. Climbing off her face, I planted myself between her legs and lightly bit her through her lacey underwear. Her hips bucked; her clit was sensitive from her own touch.

'Come for me, darling,' I crooned as I pulled down her underwear, hiked up her skirt and dived into that sweet spot that tasted of metallic honey. A groan escaped me at the taste of her. It was everything. Focusing my tongue on her clit, I watched as her hips bucked under me; she was so sensitive.

Being wet from her first orgasm, I didn't waste any time as I thrust two fingers into her, hard and deep. I withdrew them just as fast and matched the pace of her hips. She was already so close for me. I pulled my lips away, settling over her so that I could focus all of my energy into penetrating her. She whimpered for a brief moment as I drew away, but once my rhythm had picked up she was gasping—clutching at me and the couch, unable to find purchase.

'F-FUCK!' she screamed as I slammed into her one last time and curled those fingers inside of her, sending her over the peak as her body tightened and exploded in pleasure.

'Good girl.' I smirked sitting above her.

Her eyes glinted as she bit her bottom lip, calling me to drive in and out of her one more time as another gasp escaped her lips.

'Sunshine, that was everything. *You're* everything.'

# 16
# VALENTINA

Six Months Later

'I don't want to go out there. Can't we just stay here all night.' I said wrapping my arms around my wife as she fixed her hair in the mirror. She looked ethereal in her wedding dress. My legs had nearly given out as she walked towards me down that aisle only two hours ago.

'No, all of our guests are arriving and waiting for us.'

'But I behaved so well during the photos, where's my reward?' I pouted pulling her back flush against my front as I started nibbling on her ear. Her breath hitched as her eyes stuttered shut before she stepped away and turned towards me. Her crossed arms and raised brow were meant to challenge me but all it did was make me want her more. I could feel the wetness in my pants building.

'Is me being your wife, not reward enough?'

I sunk to my knees in front of her. 'You being my wife is my greatest gift, achievement and reward in this lifetime and every lifetime, Sunshine.' Her lips couldn't help but pull into that incandescent smile of hers that always had me melting in a very different way. Every emotion I felt for her prickled under the surface. She was perfection in every sense of the word, and I was humbled she had chosen *me*. Me to spend her life with. Create with. Explore this world and this life with. I didn't deserve the Goddess before me, and I would throw myself at her feet every day for the rest of my life in thanks.

'I love you.' I breathed taking her hands and pressing her palms to the sides of my face taking in her touch, I closed my eyes and settled into this moment with her. 'I'm scared.' I admitted opening my eyes. She sunk to the floor instantly in front of me.

'Why?' confusion marred that gorgeous face of hers and I needed to wipe away any feeling from it that wasn't pure unadulterated joy.

'Because I have never been happier. Promise you'll never leave me.' I said with only a hint of the desperation I was truly feeling lacing my voice.

'Did I not just vow it in front of everyone we love?' she caressed my cheek as I sunk into her touch. 'I love you V. You're my everything. Always.' Her gentle lips met mine in a chaste kiss before she pressed her forehead to mine.

'I know.' I drew as much air into my lungs as possible and expelled the doubt from every corner of my mind as I exhaled through the fear.

'What do you need me to do to prove it to you?'

'Well, since you're asking nicely, I think letting me make you come would do the trick.' She raised a brow at me and muttered something about me being insufferable or insatiable or both under her breath. She stood dragging me to the chaise, kicking off her heels with each step before hitching her silk dress higher and higher up her legs until those delicious thighs were on full display.

'Fuck me so hard, no one out there will ever doubt what

we have.' She said as she sprawled herself against the velvet fabric of the chaise. I would make her *scream.*

'You're lucky I didn't know you weren't wearing underwear, or I would've dragged you here before the ceremony even began to get a taste of you.'

'I'm wearing silk, I didn't want any lines to show.' She said as her eyes heated looking at the almost manic look in mine as I took her in.

'Hold that dress for me, Sunshine.' I said as I leaned forward and dipped my tongue into her and felt that familiar metallic tang that had me salivating for more. I wasted no time devouring her, fucking her with my tongue as my finger swirled over her clit in increasing intensity. Her hips bucked as she bit into her lip trying to stifle the yell that fought its way out. But I would have everyone here hearing my name on her lips as she climaxed.

I slipped two fingers inside her with ease, she was soaking wet for me, it drove me feral with need. Curling them up I felt the moment I hit that sweet spot inside her that had her letting go of her dress and gripping onto the chaise, fighting not to lose herself to the visceral feeling consuming her.

'Oh, fuck me.' She cursed under her breath. I wasn't sure if they were a demand or words of shock.

'Scream for me, Sunshine.'

She tried to glare at me but I just sunk deeper inside of her and replaced my tongue over her clit and watched every muscle tighten in her body as she shook. Then I pressed the tip of my tongue under the hood of her clit to the rawest part of her and watched her shatter beneath me as she screamed my name.

'V! oh my fucking god V!'

'That's more like it, Sunshine.' I pulled back fixing her

dress, watching the rise and fall of her chest as she caught her breath, her limbs lax and loose at her sides.

'Y-your turn.' She almost slurred the words as I brushed her curls from her eyes.

'I don't think you have it in you.'

'Oh, I don't, but I have something that will.' She pointed to her bag off in the corner of her room. Being the dutiful wife I got it for her. *Wife.* That word tasted almost as good as her on my tongue. How the fuck did I get so lucky.

'Put these on.' She held out a black lace pair of underwear with a vibrator in the front. Oh, she wanted to watch me squirm. Taking them, I gave her a chaste kiss on her cheek before sliding them on. I watched her watch me and it made my skin prickle with delight.

'Stop fucking and get out here.' Zane said banging on the door of the bridal suite.

We burst into laughter and fixed ourselves up for our big entrance.

Everyone cheered but I didn't see a single one as I watched the smile plastered on my girls' face. She was surrounded by people who were happy to see her succeed when her whole life she had been surrounded by those that wanted to tear her down.

We did things differently. No speeches. No MC. Just good music and good food. We didn't have a big table on a stage at the head of the room, instead we sat on a table like the others with my brothers, Matt and Ash. Her and Ash had become fast friends and were nearly inseparable. I must admit it had left me borderline bitter at times, wanting her attention all to myself but I had learned to share my world with everyone around me.

'The food is fucking fantastic, you've outdone yourself V.' Matt said between mouthfuls of the slow cooked lamb.

'She didn't cook it.' Z said attempting to joke but with his face, it came across as a threat at best. Matt choked on his food as Ash passed him a glass of scotch to wash it down.

'Really Matt, when are you doing to stop being scared of this overgrown puppy?' Xav chided shaking his head.

'When he gets a total face replacement like Nicholas Cage in Face Off.' He grumbled. I couldn't help the laugh that left me.

'Oh, come on, he's just a big softie.' Ash said picking up a dinner roll and throwing it at Zane's head. Sunshine's face emulated Matt's which was pure shock and terror. Although she had become close to my siblings her and Zane's relationship had started as a boss and employee and she found it hard to shake it at times. Ash however was fearless, the woman was a trauma surgeon, so she didn't baulk at much.

Zane chuckled before picking up a knife and aiming it at Ash always trying to one up. Matt leapt from his seat ready to take the hit should Zane throw it, but Ash raised her middle finger in challenge.

Before Zane could let the knife loose, I picked up my own and slammed it into his other hand that laid flat against the table.

'Fuck, what was that for.' He cursed ripping the blade from his hand and wrapping it in a napkin.

'Because you're acting like a child, turning a food fight into a knife fight. This is a wedding Z. Behave yourself.' Xav scolded. Matt sat back down trying to fix himself so that it didn't look like he had just been in the throes of panic. Amongst all the commotion, my beautiful little ray of Sunshine had pulled out her phone and clicked the app linked to the underwear she had made me wear.

As the vibration hit me, I gripped the table suddenly, my glass shaking. I cast a look her way, eyes wide but all I got in return was her playful grin and the level of the vibration being kicked up a notch. The conversation around me faded as I closed my eyes and tried to collect myself, actively working to reposition my limbs to sit naturally as I breathed through the intensity that was raging between my legs. I wouldn't last long. I felt as though I were being electrified as my clit felt things I didn't think were humanly possible.

'V, I'm talking to you.' Xav's words broke through the pleasure filled haze.

'Huh?'

'I was asking if you settled on your itinerary for the honeymoon yet? I know you were tossing up which country to fly to first.' We had been doing that hadn't we? But for the life of me that woman increased the level of the vibration once more, all coherent thoughts leaving me. I couldn't even tell you the name of a single country we had thought about flying to. We had been toying with the idea of flying around Europe for a year visiting galleries and immersing ourselves in the culture there. Slowing down for a moment and just basking in each other and the world around us as we sought inspiration in the countryside to the alps.

'Y-yes.' I stuttered out as I breathed through the cresting wave of pleasure. He stared at me wanting me to elaborate but I couldn't do anything but white knuckle the table and bite down on my tongue.

'S-SUNSHINE!' I screamed as the vibrations reached their peak and my pleasure erupted within me. Sunshine having mercy on me answered my brother with the most innocent grin on her face. Zane being the hawk like observer he was chuckled under his breath and shook his head while Matt made gagging sounds having finally caught on to what had just happened.

Once my breathing evened out, Ash all but stage whispered across the table.

'Send me the link to that thing.' She winked my way. I rolled my eyes turning to Sunshine, dragging her chair to mine.

'Happy now, Sunshine?' I asked my hand gripping her silk covered thigh as I watched that satisfied smirk take hold of her.

'With you? Always.'

# ACKNOWLEDGMENTS

This book would quite literally not exist without the incredible Ash or as you may know her, A.M. Nelson and Matt. It was following her hens night when I crashed her hubby's bucks that I was faced with *Sunshine*.

The first two chapters of this book are more or less how that night actually transpired and the rest of it is a fantasy that only lives within these pages.

I, of course need to thank my own husband, because my writing takes me away from him and the family when I get lost in these worlds and characters. I become transfixed, but he is ever patient, encouraging and supportive of my writing because he knows what it gives me and my soul.

I want to thank my best friend Courtney who beta read this and every book in this series. She is that no bullshit best friend who everybody needs in their corner. She reality checked me, challenged me and held my fragile author heart with such care and compassion encouraging every step of the way. She is an incredible support.

To Bonnie my editor, thank you for refining this story with me and for hyping me up when I started doubting myself.

To my ARC readers, thank you for giving my first book in this series a go when you had no reason to. I appreciate each and every one of you for the time you took out of your busy lives to read my book baby, it means the world to me.

The most important thanks are for *you*, the reader. I

cannot fathom that you picked up this book and read a piece of me. Invested time into my world and its characters when there are millions of others to choose from. I hope something in these pages resonated with you. And as always, I hope you like it but feel free to hate it.

# ABOUT THE AUTHOR

Leila Thorne is a Melbourne based indie author of dark romance with wide open door spice. She writes about women who despite their trauma and rage at the world around them, keep going. Connecting and loving even when it's terrifying to do so. When she's not writing she is walking through nature, listening to soul destroying music, thinking of the next story and where those characters will take her.

# ALSO BY LEILA THORNE

**Death and Devotion Series**

Unyielding

**Standalone**

When Darkness Reigns

www.ingramcontent.com/pod-product-compliance
Lightning Source LLC
Chambersburg PA
CBHW011928050726
47591CB00009B/2393

* 9 7 8 1 7 6 4 3 5 5 7 3 5 *